APRIL GENEVIEVE TUCHOLKE

Dial Books
an imprint of Penguin Group (USA) LLC

DIAL BOOKS
Published by the Penguin Group
Penguin Group (USA) LLC
375 Hudson Street
New York, New York 10014

USA / Canada / UK / Ireland / Australia / New Zealand / India / South Africa / China

penguin.com

A Penguin Random House Company

Library of Congress Cataloging-in-Publication Data
Tucholke, April Genevieve.
Between the spark and the burn / April Genevieve Tucholke.
pages cm
Sequel to: Between the devil and the deep blue sea.
Summary: "Seventeen-year-old Violet is looking for the boy she fell in love with last summer, the charismatic liar River West Redding, but as she scours the country for him, she begins to wonder who she's really chasing—and who she really loves"—Provided by publisher.
ISBN 978-0-8037-4047-1 (hardback)
[1. Love—Fiction. 2. Trust—Fiction. 3. Good and evil—Fiction.] I. Title.
PZ7.T7979Bew 2014 [Fic]—dc23 2013048697

Printed in the United States of America
1 3 5 7 9 10 8 6 4 2

Designed by Nancy R. Leo-Kelly
Text set in Adobe Caslon Pro

TO ALL THE REDHEADS

It was many and many a year ago,
in a kingdom by the sea,
that Annabel Lee lived with no other thought
than to love and be loved by me.

—Edgar Allan Poe

What has happened before will happen again.
What has been done before will be done again.
There is nothing new in the whole world.

—Ecclesiastes 1:9–18

Between the
Spark
and the
Burn

CHAPTER 1

MY DEAD GRANDMOTHER Freddie once told me that the Devil created all the fear in the world.

But then, the Devil once told me that it's easier to forgive someone for scaring you than for making you cry.

The problem with River West Redding was that he'd done both to me.

Since then I'd spent months just waiting. Waiting on my rotting mansion's wide front porch, on its secret little beach at the bottom of the cliffs, in its nefarious guesthouse. And I was getting antsy. I'd tasted love and terror last summer, and it left a sweetness in my mouth. I wanted to go somewhere. Anywhere. I wanted to make something happen. I wanted to get bone-shaking scared and face my fear. I wanted to get scratched. Bruised. Bloody.

River and his brother Brodie were gone. Long gone. Doing God knows what. Alone. Or together. Who knew.

Was River the Devil?

Was Brodie?

Mostly I tried not to think of them. Either of them. Of what they were up to or the trouble they were causing or the lies they were lying.

And mostly that didn't work. At all.

Where are you, River?

Silence and not a word. Not for months. Neely had gone looking, but nothing. Maybe this was a good thing. Maybe it meant River was keeping his promise. But then why hadn't he come back? He'd glowed up my damn heart last summer and then left without a trace. He'd been gone so long now that I could barely remember the smell of his skin. Or the way his eyes lit up when he lied. And lied. And lied.

River, what would you say if you could see me now, lonely little book-reading Violet, talking about getting in trouble and making something happen? Would you crooked-smile at me with that glint in your eyes and say, "I like you, Vi"? Or would you look worried and run your hands through your hair, and wonder what the hell had changed inside me since last summer?

A gust of cold wind blew in off the sea and smacked me

in the face. Instead of wincing, I smiled. I had a blanket around my shoulders, coffee in a nearby thermos, and a pair of binoculars in my hand. The sea stretched on forever before me, and my thoughts went with it.

I'd read stories of widows who never recovered from the Death at Sea of their captain husbands. Widows who spent their days wandering the seashore, waiting.

But that wasn't what I was doing down here, under the moody sky by the capering waves in the hidden little cove by my cliff-hugging tumbledown mansion that my grandmother Freddie had named Citizen Kane.

My Freddie-blue eyes squinted under the cold, glaring sun. I'd starting watching the ships again, out there on the Big Blue. I'd started wishing I was on them.

I sighed as a freezing winter breeze blew across my neck. A wave crashed into the sand and stretched its long fingers toward me. It drenched my feet and the hem of Freddie's red dress—which I had stupidly worn down to the beach when I knew better. The seawater made the dress look redder, like it was blushing.

My hands pressed into cold ground. I leaned back. Closed my eyes. The sand rubbed against the Brodie-scars on my wrists, and they started hurting. But it was a good hurt, like cold snow melting on warm skin. Or like kissing River's lips after he lied.

Maybe it was River's magic that made me think of him still. Made me talk to him like I used to talk to Freddie. Maybe it was that bit of glow still lingering in me like the last tingle of opium in an addict's blood.

River, I found something.

Heard something.

Freddie once caught me climbing a tree in the Citizen's backyard. I was twenty feet off the ground and still going up when I heard her voice. *GET DOWN RIGHT NOW, VIOLET WHITE.* The second my feet hit earth she wrapped her arms around me and hugged me for five whole minutes, maybe more.

"Your life is not your own, Vi," she said. "Don't you know that? It belongs to the people who love you. So you need to take better care of it."

Freddie was right, I supposed.

I wasn't taking very good care of my life. Not since River came into it.

And yet . . .

I walked back up the steep trail toward home, my wet dress hitting my boots with a smack, each step. And I sang a little song to myself, something that I made up as I went along, something that was melancholic and nursery rhyme, something that sounded a little bit like *A-hunting I will go, a-hunting I will go.*

CHAPTER 2

I FOUND MY parents painting out in the shed—it got great afternoon sun, even in winter, which it was. It sat there, squat and chipping paint, in its little shaft of sunshine, wedged in between the skeletal winter woods and the overgrown maze and the now empty guesthouse and the beautiful, buffeted, browbeaten, salt-stained Citizen Kane.

I loved the ocean. Its sounds were like lullabies and mothers' voices—I'd grown up on them, a soundtrack of lapping waves and seagulls and storms.

Yet the rollicking sea sea sea was a bully. I reached up to the low roof of the shed and knocked off a couple of icicles. A rotted piece of wood fell with them. I left it on the ground and went inside.

My brother was in there too, painting away, and the redheaded orphan boy, Jack. My next-door neighbor Sunshine was sitting on the floor, watching. I sat down next to her and enjoyed the cluttering bodies and the burnt smell of the space heater in the corner.

It was Christmas Eve and pretty much everyone I knew was packed into a painting shed. There wouldn't be any baking, or decorating, or caroling. Not with the Whites, not at the Citizen. But that was all right with me.

"So I've decided to go after River."

I said it quick, just like that, before I had a chance to think better of it.

"Who is River?" my mother asked, head snapping up, looking straight at me. *Really* looking, for once. Most of the time her eyes were distracted and dreamy when she talked to me, as if her mind were clicking through colors, figuring out the exact peachy shade of my skin, the perfect wheat-yellow combination of my blond hair. My parents painted and the rest of us moved around them in a blur.

"Neely's older brother," Luke said when I didn't answer. They searched my face, Luke and Jack and Sunshine, trying to puzzle out why I'd brought up River after all this time, why I'd dipped my toes into that mess of lying, glowing, out of control, brown-eyed, brown-haired rich boy.

The hell if I knew why I did it. The words just fell out of my head, out of my mouth, like leaves off trees. Like snow out of the sky.

Maybe there was something in the air.

I sighed.

I wondered if Neely would be back for Christmas.

I missed him.

I missed the way he reminded me of River—the way he drank espresso with narrowed eyes and ran his hands through his hair.

Though Neely's hair was blond, like mine, not brown, like River's.

And Brodie, the other brother, the half brother, his was red. Red, red, red.

I missed the way Neely laughed at everything. Red-headed cowboys with knives. River's lying. Everything.

I missed the way he loved his older brother so damn much and at the same time really liked putting his fists in River's face.

Neely had run off three times already, trying to find his older brother, trying not to think about his younger one.

But nothing.

I wanted Neely to come back. But not because he looked like River. And not because I was restless and cabin-fevered and dying for something to happen.

I wanted him to come back because I'd found something while he was gone.

"Violet." This from Dad, though he didn't look up from the sunset colors he was splashing on his canvas. He leaned forward on his little wooden painter's chair, his nose almost touching the wet paint, and the pink skin of his bald spot caught the winter sun coming through the shed's skylight. He motioned at me with his free hand. "Violet, fetch me the Dante."

I knew better than to ask follow-up questions when my father was painting. They wouldn't get answered, so I didn't even try.

People didn't change. Not really. Not ever.

Except . . .

Freddie changed, once. She'd given up booze and boys and trouble and painters and Reddings. I'd found the letters. I knew.

I've changed too, River. You would have noticed, if you were here, because you notice everything.

Even Luke and Sunshine were different now, after Brodie. After the bat and the rat and the cutting and the leaving me for dead. They were deeper, darker, quieter. Freddie used to say that kids were sponges, soaking up everything around them.

I wondered what I had soaked up from River last summer.

Something good.

Something bad.

Freddie would have been able to tell me.

I looked from Dad to Mom. Dad leaned forward when he was concentrating. Mom leaned back. Her straight brown hair, long like mine and Sunshine's, swished across her back as her pretty hazel eyes blinked against the bright light.

I went to the door.

"Vi."

I turned back around. My twin brother waved his fingers at me, just like dad. "Fetch me some coffee."

"Me too," Jack said from the far corner, though he at least glanced up and gave me a grin to take the edge off.

I walked up the steps of the Citizen, on my way to the library. I'd been sitting right there, right there on those steps, reading Hawthorne on a balmy, breezy June day, when I first saw River. When I first saw the wavy hair and the brown eyes and the black linen pants and the white button-down shirt and the panther hips and the all of it.

Dante. Citizen Kane's big, fat, twisty-staired dusty library was a thing to behold. The long velvet curtains hadn't been drawn to let in the sun, and the room was shadowed and cold. So cold it burned the inside of my nose. I thought about starting a fire in the fireplace—there was some old wood piled up in a nearby basket from God knew when. But as my fingertips touched the knobby bark I remembered reading a story about someone somewhere who lit a fire under a sooty chimney, breathed in, and fell over dead.

So I just stood in the icy library shadows wondering what to do, and the next thing I knew, I was shivering. And it might have been from the cold. Or it might have been that dark rooms made me think of Brodie now. Of him watching and listening and waiting, all those days last summer when we didn't know he was there.

I went to the floor-length curtains and yanked them open with both arms, dramatically, like people do in movies. Dust exploded into the air and rolled around in the pale winter light.

The world outside was still. Holding its breath, like it was waiting for snow. The pine trees were tall and green, as always, but everything else was brown and stiff and dead. The sea was calm and gray, reflecting the cloudy sky above. The broken nude fountain girls had lost their dresses of ivy, and icicles hung from their fingertips and noses and breasts.

One bold ray of sunshine shoved its way through the clouds and reached into the library, and suddenly everything inside looked comfy and cozy. The books seemed to be fidgeting in the light, as if wanting to be held. Even the ratty sofa seemed to be smiling at me, and looked like it wanted me to curl up in its arms.

I started up the spiral staircase to the poetry section, flinching when the frigid metal railing touched my palm. I found Dante's *Inferno* on the bottom shelf, the last book on the end, covered in gray dust so thick it looked like the book was wearing a wool sweater. No one had put their hands on this shelf in a while.

John White needed inspiration from Dante's description of hell, no doubt. My dad painted hell a lot. Maybe because his mother, my grandmother Freddie, had talked about the Devil all the time.

Or maybe not.

I reached for the book, and breathed in. Dust and frozen air. Hell sounded kind of good at the moment. Warm.

Sorry, Freddie.

I was glad my parents were home. Even if they'd gone to Europe for all those months, and sent no postcards, and seemed to forget us entirely, caught up in their art like a person gone stupid and selfish with their first taste of love. I was still glad to have the bastards back. I was.

I leaned over the black railing that bordered the upper level, wrapping all the way around the library. I hugged the dusty Dante to my chest, and looked down at the grand room below.

We should spend more time in here. Instead of just the kitchen and the painting shed and the attic and our bedrooms. We should try to be a family in here. It's a family kind of room.

Freddie used to end her summer nights in the library, sitting on one of the swoopy art deco sofas, reading to herself or out loud to me. In late spring it always smelled like the lilac bushes outside the windows, and I figured not even River would have nightmares if he went to sleep with the smell of those purple flowers floating in from outside . . .

My eyes shifted to the side of the room, and the thought drifted away.

I saw it.

There were sloppy stacks of books on the floor in the corner near the fireplace and the grandfather clock. They had been growing and growing over the five years since Freddie's death. One tower had collapsed onto its side and lay sprawled across the floor . . . and behind the collapsed tower was another stack of books, almost hidden in the shadows. But the shaft of winter sun hit it now in just the right place. And I saw it.

The color of green tea with cream in it.

Of moss growing up a tree.

Of Freddie's ancient ruby-eyed tiger statue carved from jade that we'd had to sell three years ago.

That specific shade of green was Freddie's favorite color. My wonderful, flawed, blue-eyed, Devil-fearing grandmother Freddie.

I'd looked for it for years . . . something that Freddie had poured her secrets into. Something that Freddie had left for me. Only me. Not Luke, not my parents. Just me. I found it last summer—letters to Freddie from Jack's grandfather, and River's too. But I didn't think that was all of it. Freddie used to read me gothic books right here in this library. Books in which characters uncovered secret diaries from departed loved ones. She had to know I would look for hers, after her death.

I dropped the Dante and took off down the spiral steps. I pushed books out of my way, reckless and stupid like a bully in the schoolyard. I reached forward, fingers grasping, grasping, and then the Freddie-green was in my hand, my palm gliding along the creamy green leather, butter-smooth.

I opened it.

Looked inside.

Saw the thick, heavy writing, as familiar to me as the tilt of her nose and the lilt of her voice.

Freddie's diary.

I'd found it, damn it all. I'd finally found it.

Merry Christmas, Violet, Freddie whispered, from wherever she was.

CHAPTER 3

September

Can still feel Will's lips on me. On my neck, stomach, back, hips, thighs . . .

The diary felt warm in my hands, like it had kept a little bit of living, breathing Freddie in it.

I was lying in River's bed, in the guesthouse. I hadn't done that in months. The lamp with its red fringe shade was shooting blood-colored slants across the bed. I could see smudges on the nightstand where my fingertips had disturbed the dust.

Freddie's diary wasn't a day-by-day-er. She listed months but not years, which fit my mysterious grandmother to a damn T. She couldn't give too much away. Even in her diary.

I'd only read the first line and already I felt filled up and ready to burst.

Will. River's grandfather. Neely's grandfather. Brodie's grandfather. I wasn't surprised that the diary opened with him. It felt like locks clicking and puzzle pieces snapping into place.

So I read the first line again.

And then again.

I couldn't seem to make myself move past it and read on.

Maybe I was a coward. A Freddie-coward. Maybe I didn't want to know this person who let boys like River's grandfather kiss her thighs.

I kept reading that one line, over and over, never getting any further, holding my breath, letting it out, holding it again, until the book floated down onto my chest, and I drifted off to sleep in between one word and the next . . .

Something banged in the kitchen. My heart jumped into my throat, the way it does when I sleep too hard and wake up too fast.

Neely?

River?

Brodie?

And then it all came back, boom, and I was there, right there, me and Brodie standing by the railroad tracks, the dead boy at our feet, Brodie's flaming red hair, tall and skinny as they come, Brodie, in the guesthouse kitchen, my blood covering his neck and shoulders, his face pushed into mine, the smell of copper and steam and madness hugging me up just as I hugged him up and Luke had the knife at Neely's throat and River just stood over the kettle of hissing water and—

I turned off the lamp. Strained forward in the dark.

Click.

Click.

It was Brodie's boot heels clicking on the floor. It was.

I put my hands to my face and my screams were as silent as the moonlight cutting across the end of the bed.

And then I stopped.

I threw back the blankets. I was done silent-screaming. If it was Brodie, then he'd get me no matter where I was, so I might as well meet him standing up.

Besides, I'd asked for this. I'd wanted something to happen. And now it had.

I went to the kitchen, feeling my way down the dark hall.

Click.

Click.

The guesthouse kitchen was empty, no one, not a soul, no moka pot on the stove, no cups in the sink, no smell of coffee in the air, no tall boy in the shadows.

The wind was beating on the kitchen shutters, making the latches shake. That's all it was.

I breathed out. And in.

I'd been ready to meet him. Hadn't I?

I opened the windows. It was black, all black, outside. A storm was brewing out on the ocean. I could smell it more than see it, smell the sea being stirred up, pushing salt into the air. Maybe we were finally going to get some snow.

I pulled my cardigan tighter. The guesthouse had heating, and was one-tenth the size of Citizen Kane, with lower ceilings, so it was actually warmer sleeping here than in my own bed. But then I usually wrecked it all by opening the windows to let the sea air in.

I looked around the kitchen.

One boy. Coffee. Lies.

Two boys. Coffee. Fighting.

Three boys. A knife. And blood, blood, blood, blood, blood.

A snowflake blew in through the window. It floated up, and then twirled down to land on my cheek.

≈≈≈

I felt the heat first. Before the fingers, and the palm. It permeated my dream, warmth pouring down my back and making me shiver with the goodness of it in the cold, cold room.

"Vi, wake up."

I pushed my eyelids open. Neely's hand was on my upper back. I turned over, and his hand moved to the pillow beside me.

"Neely," I whispered.

"Hey," he said, and smiled, ear to ear, his eyes glinting so bright I could see them even in the dark.

A pause.

"Did you find him?" I asked, already knowing the answer.

He shook his head. "It was just a bunch of bored, lying kids with some mischief to burn off. *Evil fairies prey on small Connecticut town* . . . It was a long shot. I should have known better. Tabloids."

He laughed.

I slid over and Neely stretched himself out on the bed beside me. We both stared up at the dark ceiling.

"It's cold in here," he said.

"It's Christmas Eve," I said back. "December. Maine. Notorious."

"Yeah, but that radiator over there is clinking and clanking away. No, it's cold in here because you opened the windows like someone with a death wish."

"That too."

Neely laughed again and it was low and rumbling and

chuckling and made me want to laugh right along with him. He lifted his arm and pressed something on his wrist. His watch lit up. "Eleven thirty. Almost Christmas Day."

I turned my head and looked at him. "Merry Christmas, Neely."

He grinned. "I got you something."

"A present?"

"Yeah."

"No you didn't."

"Yes I did."

"But I didn't get you anything."

"That's okay."

"Well then, give it here." I was grinning right back at him.

"No way. You'll get it later, when we open presents with everyone else. You guys put up a tree like I told you to?"

I shook my head, and my hair rustled against the pillow.

He sighed. "Fine. This morning we're getting a tree. First thing. All you have to do is walk into the woods past your backyard, and chop. Throw some lights on it. It's not hard. You're worthless, all you little Rembrandts. Get your head out of your paints. Christmas comes but once a year."

I reached up and turned on the lamp by the bed. Neely jumped into focus. Blond hair, the roots a bit darker now that they weren't bleached white by the sun. Big smile.

Beaming blue eyes. Broken nose. Tall and long next to me on the bed. No bruises. At least not where I could see them. He hadn't been fighting, then.

Good.

It was nice to see him again. It really, really was.

"Want some coffee?" I asked.

He nodded, looking at me in the same pleasant way I was looking at him.

Freddie's diary was still lying on the bed. I moved it to the nightstand. I wasn't ready to tell Neely about it yet. Not him, not Luke, not anyone.

I buttoned my yellow cardigan over my long white nightgown—the one Luke hated, because he said it made me look like a wailing Victorian ghost—and then put on a pair of striped wool socks to counteract the freezing floor. Neely was already in the kitchen, warming up the moka pot and pulling down espresso cups from the cupboard.

I watched him as he poured the steaming coffee. I breathed in the salty sea air and the roasty toasty espresso and the clean soft smell of falling snow. The flakes were blowing in stronger now, dancing around Neely's head. He handed me a cup and I sipped the coffee, slow, and looked around the guesthouse.

It still had the chipped teacups and the yellow cupboards and the patchwork quilts and the paintbrushes drying on the counter and the tubes of paint scattered on tables and windowsills. But all of them meant something more to me now. Things had happened here. Important things. Kissing and lying and cooking and cutting. The guesthouse would never just be the guesthouse again.

"What are you doing?" Neely asked.

I'd finished the joe, turned on one of the dim kitchen lights, and started digging around in the closet by the front door.

"Here it is."

"Here's what?"

I looked at Neely over my shoulder. He was leaning one hip into the kitchen counter in the same graceful way that River used to. He was barefoot too, even with the cold, and he had the same pretty feet as his older brother.

A snowflake flew in and landed on the top of his left foot, right on the smooth skin at the base of his big toe. And something about it, about the snowflake melting gently on his pretty Redding foot, made my stomach flutter.

I turned back to the closet. "I found this when I was looking for the Citizen's blueprints last summer—we never did find that secret passageway . . ." I pulled the brown wooden box out, stood up, and brought it to the table.

"That thing is never going to work," Neely said.

I picked up the frayed old cord, plugged it in, and static filled the kitchen.

"You were saying?"

Neely laughed.

"I've been listening to the radio a lot since you left. Something about hearing things from the wider world . . ." I paused. "It's been appealing to me. I was fiddling with the vintage Freddie radio in my bedroom one night, looking for this AM station that plays *War of the Worlds* every Saturday. But what I found was this."

I spun the dial, right, left, right again, and there it was. A man's voice, deep and cultivated like Orson Welles's, speaking of, started rolling over us.

Hey there, believers. It's Wide-Eyed Theo. I'm here. You're here. And it's the witching hour. That means it's time for your daily dose of Stranger Than Fiction. *Are you ready?*

First of all, Merry Christmas to those out there who still honor the conventional holidays. Good for you. And in the spirit of festive things, our top story tonight comes from a woman in Toronto who claims that a man calling himself "Father Christmas" has been visiting her each year on Christmas Eve since she was fifteen. He's attractive, bearded, and in his mid-forties. He doesn't seem to age. According to her, she wakes up to find him standing over her bed. They share one loving night, and he's gone the next morning. The woman's husband, who sleeps in the bed next to her, has never woken up during the visit, and seems not to . . .

And then. The part I was waiting for. The part I wanted Neely to hear.

. . . Last but not least, I mentioned the other night that a small community in the Appalachian Mountains has been seeing, quote, "a boy with flames in his eyes and hooves instead of feet." This is all I've got, so if you can make something of it, then you're smarter than me. But I'm going to squeeze my source for more info tomorrow. Stay tuned.

I clicked the radio off. "Well? Is there anything to it? It's got to be better than the tabloids, right? A boy with devil-feet? That could be something. It could."

Neely looked at me. "River's been gone for months. I've always been able to track him down before, Vi, but now . . . nothing. No stories, not even in the local papers. No one is talking. Maybe it means River's just hiding out somewhere and not using the glow." Neely paused for a long second. "Still, for some reason, I'm starting to get . . . frantic."

Neely didn't look frantic, standing there, all tall and smiling with that chipper gleam in his eyes that said I'm-one-second-away-from-laughing.

Freddie used to say there were many ways to lie, and most didn't use your mouth.

I wrapped my hand around Neely's arm, the one with the scar.

"We'll find him," I said.

Neely put his hand on mine. "I know. It's just . . . what kind of shape will he be in when we do? I have a bad feeling, Vi."

A cold wind burst in through the window, and we both shivered.

"Maybe he's just holed up in some pleasant place like Quebec City," I whispered. What is it about snow in the middle of the night that makes you want to whisper? "We'll find him wearing a red knit scarf and he'll speak flawless French and eat poutine every day for lunch."

"Yeah," Neely whispered back at me, not smiling now. "But I doubt it."

I hugged him then, hugged him up hard, like I'd been wanting to do since I first saw him. Because I doubted it too.

Standing there in the kitchen with the smell of coffee and the cold and the snow and Neely's arms tight around me, all I could hear was the little voice inside my heart that whispered, *None of this is going anywhere good, anywhere good at all . . .*

CHAPTER 4

FIRST THING, NEELY woke us kids up at dawn, just as the first pink was squeezing into the winter sky. He made us all march through the fresh fallen snow in Citizen Kane's backyard to get a Christmas tree.

Sunshine had a thick blue hat pulled down over her long brown hair, and her brown eyes were clear and lazy. Whether Neely fetched her at the Black family cabin down the road, or whether he'd found her in Luke's bed, I didn't know. Sunshine's parents, Cassie and Sam, were already used to their only child spending most of her time at our house, so I guess the transition to her dating my brother had been pretty easy.

Luke looked happy. He carried an ax in one hand, and Sunshine's fingers in the other. The early-morning light brought the red out in his hair, and Jack's too.

Jack was singing a song about snow that he made up as he went along. The serious, quiet Jack I'd known last summer, the one who organized those kids in the cemetery to fight the Devil, the one who'd been tied up in the Glenship attic, the one who had his back sliced up by Brodie's knife . . . he was pretty much gone.

Jack was still serious when he painted, but otherwise . . . I guess life at Citizen Kane suited him. Now he was all about running around the house for no particular reason other than the joy of doing it. Or making "forty-ingredient sandwiches" in the kitchen with Luke, and then daring him to take the first bite. Or drinking too much coffee too late at night and then jumping up and down on one of the guest beds for twenty minutes, begging me to join him.

My parents accepted Jack into their life, as if he'd always been there. As if they'd always had an eleven-year-old son and just forgot about him for a while.

I never told them Jack was their nephew. Half nephew. Or that Freddie had an affair with a painter and it led to my father. Or that my father had a drunk brother who wasn't a great guy and was dead now anyway so what did it matter. Maybe I would tell them one day, but I hadn't yet.

Luke and Jack picked out the tree, a straight pine, just

taller than Neely, and started chopping. Snow fell on them from the branches above and they laughed. Sunshine was by my side, drinking coffee from a thermos Neely offered her. Neely put his arm around my shoulder in a companionable way and the tree fell over into a cloud of fresh snow like a spoon dropped in a bowl of powdered sugar.

Neely had come home for Christmas and I was about as happy as I was going to get, all things considered.

≈

Roaring fire in the library. Check. Tree decked to the nines with glass ornaments found in the attic. Check. Blizzard smashing the world up outside. Check. Sunshine's parents cooking for everyone in the Citizen's big kitchen. Check.

My own parents set aside their paints for the night and Mom dug up some crispy yellowed sheet music from somewhere and we sang about the holly and the ivy and the three ships sailing in and the feast of Stephen. We ate juicy organic ham with mustard and maple syrup, and buttery potatoes, and spindly baby parsnips, and roasted chestnuts, and brown beer gingerbread. We drank spiced apple cider and hot buttered rum.

And then we opened gifts. I got a new knit scarf, black with white stripes, from Cassie, Sunshine's mother. Sunshine gave me a classic novel about one boy's journey of impossible coincidences and random fornications. My parents gave me a bottle of perfume, the same Freddie used to wear, brought to me all the way from Paris. Luke gave Jack his own set of paintbrushes, brand-spanking-new, and I gave them both a screen printing kit, which seemed to excite them in exactly the way I hoped it would.

And so on. Though I didn't see Neely's present, the one he said he'd gotten for me, and I'd been looking forward to it too.

After sunset the blizzard blew away again, and we all went outside to see the sea and the stars. The snow pressed in around our ankles and the sky went on forever and I sort of thought, *This is a pretty good day.*

The adults played cards at a card table rustled up from the cellar. *My* parents, playing cards just like normal parents, though my father had always said card games were for children and halfwits. Sunshine's mother and father sat with their skinny behinds on the edge of their chairs, and took the game very seriously, with Cassie calling for breaks every forty minutes so she could brew up more Darjeeling. She grew up in England and ran on tea like River and Neely ran on coffee.

Eventually I followed Neely into the kitchen and watched him put thick chunks of dark chocolate in a pot, add some whole milk, and some maple syrup, and melt it all until it was steaming. He spiced it with cinnamon, and a pinch of chili powder, and a shot of espresso, and poured it into an old stainless steel thermos. And then we tromped up the three flights of stairs to the Citizen's cluttered, dusty, beautiful attic.

"You look pretty," Jack said to me as he sipped from his mug of chocolate, the steam making his cheeks pink.

He was nestled into his usual place, right up next to me on one of the old sofas. He had on the black hand-knit sweater he'd gotten from Cassie, and my new black-and-white scarf, because it was freezing. Silver-white frost blossomed across the round windows, and the air was light and sharp. Luke had plugged in the space heater, but it hadn't worked its magic yet.

"You do look pretty," Neely said, sitting down on my other side. "Your blue eyes look bluer in the cold. Did you know that?"

"Freddie's eyes were like that too," Luke said. He glanced between Neely and me and looked kind of snappy and smart-alec for a second, like he knew something I didn't.

But the hell if I was going to ask him about it.

"I painted a portrait of Freddie once, outside on a bright day in February." Luke's expression went a bit deep and distant. "I was just a kid, but I remember how hard it was to mix the blue for her eyes—it was the color of the ocean and the sky and . . . every color in between, somehow."

I smiled at him. "Luke, you get so poetic when you talk about art. It almost makes you likable."

Sunshine grinned. She leaned back into my brother, and he tucked a blanket around both of them and then his distant look went away.

"You know what makes you almost likeable, Vi?" he asked. "When you forget to act smarter than everyone else for half a second. When you stop being eccentric long enough for a person to get a word in edgewise. When you stop wearing our dead grandmother's clothes and put on something that doesn't smell like dust and closet."

Sunshine laughed her throaty laugh. "I do like your new dress, Vi. We were all sick of seeing you in a dead person's clothes."

My dress was silky and long and black and came with a smooth, pale yellow cardigan that had small pearl buttons. My mother had bought it in NYC during my father's art show in October and given it to me for Christmas. I ran my hands over the skirt again. I liked the way it slid back and forth against my cold thighs, soft as air. I probably should have been saving it for a special occasion, because I didn't get new clothes very often, but what the hell.

I heard the grandfather clock in the library chime—it

sounded quiet and gentle from this far away, like it didn't want to wake anyone up. The clock had been in the house since the beginning. It broke years ago, and stayed that way until Jack went and fixed it with nothing but a wrench, a screwdriver, and a positive attitude. That kid was smart as hell and twice as charming.

I looked down at his freckled face and his auburn head. He was trying to stay up late like the rest of us, but his eyes were doing that squinting thing that always gave him away—even though Neely had put that streak of espresso in the hot chocolate. Jack yawned, and huddled down farther into the couch, and his long hair stuck out wild and frantic above his head. I figured I should probably try to cut it soon, if he'd let me.

I sighed, and then squeezed out from between Jack and Neely. Cold attic air hit me and I winced.

I'd brought the old guesthouse radio up earlier and now I set it on a table by the sofa and looked for a plug-in. I found one of River's little origami creatures hidden behind the couch as I was digging around back there for an outlet. Another hundred-dollar bill, folded in the shape of a turtle. My fingers closed around it and the River-missing feeling came back, just for a second. It was sharp and strong and unmistakable, like the smell of freshly brewed coffee.

"What are you doing over there?" Neely was watching me from the sofa, his eyes half closed, sleepy, sleepy. "Come back. It's cold over here and you're warm."

I put the turtle in my yellow cardigan's pocket, gave Neely a quick smile, and turned the knobs on the radio.

Static, static, static . . . and there it was.

Hello all ye believers of the strange and true. It's Wide-Eyed Theo. I'm here. You're here. It's the witching hour and time for your daily dose of Stranger Than Fiction. *I hope you all made merry today and are full of good cheer and well-being. Feel free to curse a scrooge, any of you that are into the bewitching arts . . .*

"What the hell is this, Vi?" Luke talked right over Theo like he didn't give a damn that I was trying to hear.

"Shut up and listen, Luke."

Luke shut up and we listened to tales of a pack of teenage grave robbers and a woman who thought she was a cat and a boy who claimed he could see the future.

And then . . .

. . . the small town in the Appalachian Mountains continues to be plagued by "a boy with flames in his eyes and hooves instead of feet." I received an update on this today. Apparently this devil-boy commands a flock of ravens, and sneaks into the bedrooms of sleeping adolescent girls to steal their dreams. His birds attack anyone who intervenes. My source wishes to remain anonymous, as the locals are a superstitious

sort with, quote, "little trust in each other and even less in the law."

If any of my listeners has an itch for adventure, I would like to direct you to Inn's End, Virginia. If you can find it. It's not listed on any maps, being "too out of the way and too full of misanthropes," according to my source.

A devil-boy with fiery eyes and goat feet, stealing dreams. If you can believe that, people. And you should, because you're believers.

It's Wide-Eyed Theo, signing off for the night.

Go forth and find the strange.

"That's it," I said, looking straight at Neely just as he looked straight at me. "Theo mentioned it three times now. It's got to mean something. This is the one."

Luke raised his eyebrows, cocky and scornful, and Sunshine looked at the opposite wall and wouldn't meet my gaze.

But Neely just grinned, and shrugged.

≈≈≈

Neely didn't go off to the guesthouse afterward, and neither did I. He crashed on the faded art deco sofa in my bedroom, and I didn't say boo, because I was fired up about the devil-boy story and didn't feel like being alone, and besides, who cared anyway.

Before Neely fell asleep, he came and sat on the end of

my bed. He pulled something from his pocket and then opened his hand. A necklace of small jade beads sat on his palm. He lifted my hair, slid the chain underneath, and clasped it shut.

"Merry Christmas, Vi."

I touched the warm green stones. Jade green. Freddie's favorite color.

"Don't even try to give it back. It's yours and you will keep it." Neely's eyes were gleaming with high spirits and a late-night shot of hot buttered rum and not-taking-no-for-an-answer.

A minute or so passed with neither of us talking, and me just running my fingers over the necklace and smiling, and Neely just sitting there looking at the necklace and me behind it, like it pleased him in some deep way.

"I found Freddie's diary," I said then, since I had to tell someone.

"Where was it?"

"Buried in the stack of books on the library floor. Probably been there since she died. I would have found it years ago if I'd ever bothered to put those books away."

Neely laughed. "That'll teach you." He reached for my hand and then turned it over and started rubbing his thumb over the center of my palm, softly, slowly, as if he wasn't sure he should be doing it.

"I haven't read it yet," I said. "The diary, I mean. I couldn't bring myself to get past the first line."

"You will," he answered. Quiet.

"Neely," I said, after a moment. "If I keep sitting here in Citizen Kane, staring at the sea and doing nothing about anything, I'll go mad. A devil-boy with fiery eyes, stealing dreams . . . That sounds like as good a lead as any. I say we take it. And this time I want to come with."

Neely was quiet for a bit. Then: "You have, what, a week before school starts again?" he asked, not looking at me, still rubbing my palm.

I nodded. I listened to his breathing until his eyes met mine. "Violet, do you ever wish that you'd never met my brother? That he'd never come here, that he'd never glowed you up in the first place and started this whole thing?"

"All the time. All the damn time, Neely." I paused. "But I'm still going with. I want to find River. And Brodie. Both. I want to do something. Anything. I miss River. I worry about him. Sometimes I think about—I remember . . ."

I didn't finish my sentence and Neely didn't make me. He just dropped my hand, went over to the sofa, slipped off his shoes, and tucked himself in.

"Neely?"

"Yeah?"

"Do you think River ever told the truth? Like when he said my sleeping next to him kept his nightmares away? Or when I held him in the attic, and he told me about your mother dying? It wasn't all just lies and glow, right?"

Neely laughed, a whispery, nighttime laugh. "Not even a liar lies all the time, Vi."

A few minutes passed.

"Night, Neely."

"Night, Violet."

I didn't fall asleep, though. My mind raced with thoughts of devil-boys and heroes and River and not-River. I picked up Freddie's diary and started to read. My new necklace kissed the skin of my neck, and Neely's soft breaths whispered to me from across the room.

This time I got a whole lot further than the first sentence.

> *September*
>
> *Can still feel Will's lips on me. On my neck, stomach, back, hips, thighs.*
>
> *If his burn is bad, if he is bad, then why does he feel so good?*
>
> *It wasn't the first time. I can't talk about the first time yet. Because it all happened, everything all at once—the burn, the pain, the pleasure, the fear—and it's still jumbled up inside of me. I was*

a fairy-tale girl locked in a tower, waiting for the white knight to save her, but taking the first burned-up boy that came along.

Glenship Manor. The library. The smell of books mixing with the smell of Will. His brown-sugar-scented slicking-back pomade. The citrus-smelling cologne he slapped on his beautiful face. The sea salt deep in his skin.

Lucas's steps. While we were behind the green curtains. I knew it was him. I knew it by the way he walked. Soft, but determined. If he'd guessed where we were, and what we were doing, he was smart enough to leave it alone. He was smart enough to know he didn't want to know.

Lucas.

Lucas.

Your love is gentle. Gentle as cool night breezes on hot skin. I wish I could absorb your gentle love and send it right back to you. But I can't.

I knew Will Redding would be beautiful. He was pretty at fifteen, prettier than me. But then he grew, and his soft angles sharpened. And now looking at him . . . I almost hate him, he's so damn breathtaking.

He's using the burn more and more. It's

stealing his mind, his wits, his sanity, bit by bit. I feel the loss of them, small but tangible, like a missing button in the middle of a shirt.

What will happen if he doesn't stop? If we don't stop?

But then he kisses me, and I stop caring.

Even when he's done kissing me, sometimes I still don't care, not for hours.

Or days.

I'd do it again. I'd do it this minute if he asked me. With or without his burn.

I don't even care.

October

Chase never knew, about Will, and the burn. Not for certain. Though if he'd been observant, like Lucas, he would have guessed that All Was Not Right. But paying close attention had never been Chase Glenship's strong point.

One brisk, clear night, Chase and Will had some of their friends up from New York City—other Bright Young Things. They came up on the train and we threw an All Hallows' Eve party. The moon was big and fat and full and orange-er than pumpkins. Its bright glow made the night midnight blue, instead of boring old black. We ignored the Glenship's electricity and lit hundreds of candles until the swanky ole place was singing with light, all the long, tall windows glowing like the harvest moon above.

We dressed in costumes and painted the subterranean walls of the Glenship. In the lower levels, off the stone tunnels that led to the swimming pool and the bowling alley, there was a nothing room with no purpose. We splashed paint and filled up every last corner with green, blue, white, yellow, red, orange, black. Chase set up his Ouija board and gave us all the heebie-jeebies when he called up the spirits and they answered. Everyone went mad with fear and ran around howling with it. I gave myself up to three Aviations before the gin took hold and I fell into the pool. Lucas rescued me, but it was Will who helped me out of my wet clothes and into bed.

I loved him. God help me, I loved him more than a girl has ever loved a boy. More than anyone has ever loved anyone.

I slid out of bed. I grabbed a flashlight from my dresser, climbed the stairs to the third floor, went past Luke's bedroom, and entered the former-ballroom-now-an-art-gallery. I went first to the painting of my grandfather, and switched on the flashlight. It was the flower-lapel-cigar portrait. Once upon a time I thought I looked like Lucas White. Just a little bit. I'd go to the ballroom and stare at him and the proud way he tilted his chin . . . I tilted my chin up just like that. Didn't I? I had that same noble gaze. Didn't I?

But then I found some letters last summer, letters to Freddie, and learned some things about my grandmother, about her affair with an auburn-haired painter, and I guess those similarities between Lucas White and me were just the imaginings of an ex-wealthy, ex-grandmothered girl hoping to find blood and clan and kinship where none actually existed.

It took me a few minutes to find the other painting. A Freddie nude, an early one. She sat on the floor, one leg up and one elbow on her bent knee, looking directly at the viewer. I hadn't been able to place the background before—it wasn't the Citizen, or the guesthouse.

Two men stood near her, fully clothed. I'd never known who they were, until now. I stood on tiptoe and grasped at the bottom of the frame with my fingertips until I got it off the wall. Then I sat down on the ballroom floor and held the square, fifteen-by-fifteen-inch frame in my lap.

The setting was the Glenship attic. I was sure of it. I'd been inside Glenship Manor since I'd last taken a good look at this picture. The abandoned mansion was full of dust and dirt and cobwebs, but you could still see it, see its grandness, like the Citizen's. The way it stood arrogantly at the other edge of town, near the sea, like it had been cast off by Echo but couldn't have cared less, hadn't even noticed, in fact.

Yes . . . I was sure. That was the attic. The pointed roof. The heavy wooden beams. The air of architectural confidence.

One of the boys in the painting was Chase Glenship. Tall. Delicate, aristocratic features. An unruly look in his eyes. He was the boy that River and Neely's grandfather Will Redding had wanted Freddie to marry . . . even though Will Redding had been in love with Freddie himself.

Chase was also the bright-eyed eldest son who had killed a girl in the Glenship cellar with a knife. That girl had been Rose Redding, Will's sister. River and Neely's great-aunt. She was only sixteen when she died.

Rose was buried in my family's mausoleum in the Echo cemetery. That had been Freddie's doing.

My grandmother's life had more twists and turns and tangles than even I'd guessed. And I'd known her better than anybody.

Hadn't I?

I leaned over the painting, so close that my nose almost touched Freddie's bare torso. A lean boy with wavy brown hair and brown eyes stood next to Chase. Will Redding. He had a straight nose and a crooked smile and he looked so much like River that it made me feel melancholy.

It had all happened before. And it would all happen again.

Where had I heard that line before?

Some fairy tale, maybe.

CHAPTER 5

THE NEXT MORNING I told Luke and Sunshine that Neely and me were going Devil hunting in Virginia.

"Devil hunting. Right." Luke smirked at me and sipped at his cup of steaming espresso. "As if that devil-boy story is true, sister. You just want to go on a road trip with Neely. Well, I want to go on a road trip too. Don't you, Sunshine?"

Sunshine's eyes went from Luke, to me, to Neely. And then she . . . fidgeted. Sunshine never fidgeted. But here she was, shifting from one foot to the other. "A winter road trip sounds fun. But I . . . I don't want to hunt any devils."

Luke set his cup down, reached forward, and pulled Sunshine into him. "There aren't any devils. Vi is being melodramatic and paranoid and we are all humoring her because that's what you do to crazy people."

I opened my mouth—

But Neely put his hand on my arm, and shook his head.

Sunshine was looking up at my brother, her eyes wide instead of hooded and sleepy like usual. Then she smiled her old, lazy smile. "All right," she said. "A road trip does sound like fun. And I'll do anything to help out my poor, mad friend Violet."

And even though Sunshine was smiling, I still saw it. The flicker behind her eyes.

I had a feeling Sunshine would regret her decision to come with, down the road. But it was her choice, and I let her make it.

It was fourteen hours to Virginia and we would take Neely's car. We would avoid the cities and spend one night on the road in the cold wilds of southeastern New York.

I wasn't even worried.

About what we would find, I mean.

I just wanted to do something. Go somewhere. Anywhere.

That's the kind of person I'd become.

≈

I stood outside in the snow as Luke and Sunshine loaded Neely's new BMW with gear cobbled together from the Citizen's cellar and Sunshine's house. I slipped in my brown suitcase—an old one of Freddie's—and a snow shovel, and a filled-to-the-brim picnic basket. We were going to camp. Yes, camp. Neely's father had frozen his credit cards and checking account in a failed attempt to get him to come home, and all I had was the origami money River had left me for a rainy day. There would be no four-star hotels for us.

Not that they had those where we were headed, anyway.

My parents came out to tell us good-bye. Luke said we were going to Virginia to inspire the muse, and they asked no follow-up questions, which was typical. Sunshine's parents put up more of a fight, one with quotes and big words and bookish hues, which was also typical.

Sam: "Sunshine, peanut, you are unaccustomed to traversing the wider world unaccompanied. While travel is fatal to prejudice, bigotry, and narrow-mindedness, as the wise man Twain once said, I still believe you are too young to go romping about in foreign places by yourself."

Sunshine: "Dad, you are being very condescending."

Cassie: "*Nuns fret not at their convent's narrow room, and hermits are contented with their cells.* William Wordsworth. A brilliant man."

Sunshine (batting her sleepy eyes): "Mom, I don't even know where to start with that one."

A pause.

Sunshine: "*Two roads diverged in a wood and I, I took the*

road less traveled by. And that has made all the difference."

Sam, to Cassie: "We've created a monster."

Sunshine sealed the deal by telling them the road trip was for "personal edification about the Civil War" and they backed right down. Sunshine had never been very scholarly, but her parents were both librarians and readers and knowledge-seekers, and she knew how to hit them where it counted.

Jack was still sulking in his room. We weren't letting him come with. I wasn't going to put him within a hundred miles of Brodie, or anything that sounded like it could be Brodie. Not on my life. But at the last minute he ran down the steps of Citizen Kane and threw himself into my arms in a giant bear hug.

I was going to miss the kid, damn it.

Luke tried to take the front seat, but Sunshine made him get in the back with her. So I got to be up with Neely. I waved good-bye to Jack and my parents and the snow-covered fountain girls and the frostbitten Citizen Kane. The wheels beneath me crunched over snow and gravel. We turned out of the driveway, and it began.

River, I'm leaving the sea. Can you even picture me without the ocean nearby? We're going to Virginia. Maybe you're there right now. Maybe you're glowing up all of Inn's End even though you promised not to. We'll find you in a cemetery, making a group of kids see dragons or witches or madmen, and then Neely and you will get into a fight and then me and you will get into a fight . . . But then we'll both forgive you because we always do. You'll make espresso and tell me some lie about how you own an island in the middle of the ocean where children run wild and live on nothing but coffee beans and I'll half believe you and then you'll lean over and kiss my neck and I won't care about anything anymore.

We listened to Billie Holiday and Skip James and Robert Johnson and Elizabeth Cotten and Mississippi John Hurt, and the white snow and brown, bony trees went on and on.

When we started curving away from the coast, I felt it. The tug that meant I was leaving the sea behind.

Freddie took Luke and me on a trip to Montreal when I was little. She went to visit an old friend and we were taken along to "experience some culture." I remember feeling the tug back then too, when we started going inward . . . like the moon pulling in the tides. If you're born near the sea, you're bound to it for life, I guess.

We stopped in a couple of quiet small towns to stretch our legs. We ate lunch sitting on the freshly shoveled steps of a small white church in some quaint Connecticut town. The sun was shining and it wasn't as cold as it could have been—it was warmer away from the ocean. I'd packed a lot of food in the large wicker picnic basket. Butter and radish sandwiches, and olives, and Gouda, and dark chocolate, and apples and pears, and all sorts of things. We cut pomegranates in half and ate the tart seeds with some of the small spoons that were strapped to the lid.

"This is fine Devil-hunting food, sis," Luke said, and laughed. "I'll be ready to take on any number of hoof-footed devil-boys, after this."

"It's not a joke," I said, though I kind of felt like it was. There was something so impulsive, so careless, about picking up and going after the missing Redding boys based on nothing but some story on a late-night radio show. "River could be there. It could be him. This is as good a lead as any. Better than the tabloids, because the stories came from real people, not hack journalists. And even if it's not River, it could still be Brodie. Odds are it's probably one of them."

Sunshine jerked when I said Brodie's name, and dropped her pink-red apple in the snow.

Brodie had made me take off my shirt and kiss him like I meant it and stand still while he slit my wrists and left me for dead. But Sunshine . . . Having your own sparked-up parents take a bat to your head, and beat you into a coma . . . that probably did something bad to a person, deep down inside.

Sunshine must have felt pretty sure we wouldn't find Brodie in Virginia, or she never would have come along.

"Don't listen to Vi," Luke said, sliding his arm around Sunshine's hips and picking her apple out of the snow. "She'll believe anything."

I scowled at that and Neely laughed. We sat in snowy silence for a few more minutes, and then Luke pulled Sunshine to her feet. They headed to the little cemetery by the church and began to point out the cool old names on the stones as they walked by.

I finished my pomegranate just as the bells started chiming above me. A sweet older couple walked by, all dressed up in their warm winter finery.

I looked over at Neely, and he had a glint in his blue eyes. It wasn't the "I'm up to no good" one that he shared with his older brother. It was a worried glint. An "I'm thinking a lot but saying little" glint.

But when Neely opened his mouth, all he said was, "I wish I had some coffee."

He'd already finished off the thermos that we'd brought. I shrugged at him, and then he looked at me and smiled his Neely smile. His blond hair was blowing in the chilly breeze, as was mine. He had on a chunky brown sweater and expensive dark trousers, and was just sitting on the steps with an earth-green scarf around his neck, looking like he was posing for the cover of a magazine called *Wintry Rich Boys*.

I sat there a minute longer on the steps, and that was all it took for the restless feeling to start crawling up my insides again.

"Hey," I shouted at Luke and Sunshine. *"It's time to go hunt some devils."*

A local heard me as he was passing by, and raised his white eyebrows at me, but I just smiled at him until he smiled back.

I slid my mittens on—another gift from Sunshine's mom—and packed up the lunch. I didn't have the heart to throw the used-up pomegranate halves away. They looked so pretty, the bright coral color against the white snow. So I left them turned upside down by the church steps.

≈

It was cold. So damn cold.

We had three tents. Luke and Sunshine were sharing one and Neely and me had the other two. We were in a tree-filled campground somewhere north of Washington Irving territory. I was surprised it was even open—we were the only people there except for a shy caretaker in a small cabin near the entrance.

It was cold. But the stars were amazing.

Sunshine built the fire, and it roared out its voice into

the quiet black night. Sunshine and I had gone camping a few times since the summer—after Brodie she'd begun to take an interest in the natural world and she'd started teaching herself wilderness survival. There was some correlation, I supposed, between what happened to Sunshine last summer, and her need to stare Mother Nature in the face. But she never spoke about any of it, not to me, so what did I know.

We sat on logs to keep ourselves out of the snow, and talked about little things like constellations and scary campfire stories from our childhoods. Our backs faced the dark and shivered, while our fronts faced the fire and glowed with warmth.

I pulled out Freddie's diary and started reading. Luke asked me what the hell it was, mainly because he was bored and probably hoped it was some torrid romance he could tease me about.

"It's my diary," I told him, making sure to meet his eyes so he wouldn't think I was lying. "Oscar Wilde said he never traveled without his because one should always have something sensational to read." I paused. "It's mainly a series of sonnets and free verse about my feelings for River . . . how our first kiss felt and how much I loved it when he held me in his arms. Things like that."

Luke squinted his eyes and folded his mouth into

an expression of pity mixed with disgust. And then he dropped the subject.

Neely knew I was lying, but he didn't flinch or wink or do one damn thing to give me away, bless his heart.

I'd shown Luke Freddie's letters last summer, after everything had quieted down. And it had kind of destroyed him for a while. I hadn't guessed how much he'd relied on her being everything he thought she was. He marched around the house and sulked for a good week. He even put away the small portrait he'd done of Freddie three years before she died. The one he'd always kept in his bedroom.

But at the end of the week it was back up again.

No, I wasn't going to tell him about the diary.

Before we went to sleep we crawled into the car so we could listen to *Stranger Than Fiction* with the heat cranked. But there was nothing of interest—an update on the teenage grave robbers in California, and two boys in Alaska who said their mother was in love with the ghost of a gold rusher who haunted their house.

"I'd rather be in California, looking for some corpse stealers," Sunshine said, after I turned off the radio. "It would be warmer. And there would be wine. California is full of wine. Besides, grave-robbing is more interesting than dream-stealing mountain boys."

"Robbers or devil-boys, what difference does it make?"

Luke tugged his wool coat tighter across his big, stupid pecs, and buttoned it up to the top. "It's just lies, anyway. All we're going to find in Inn's End is some backward town with no plumbing where the prettiest girl is the one with all her teeth. Count on it."

Neely grinned. "You know, I once heard a story that kids in a town named Echo were hunting the Devil in the local cemetery."

"I heard that story too," I said, staring Luke down, rubbing it in. "Turns out it wasn't really a lie."

My brother's eyes narrowed, but he didn't answer. He opened the car door and got out. The cold wind burst in and I shivered so hard I bit my tongue.

We left the fire blazing when we went to bed, and I huddled in my sleeping bag, watching the flames dancing outside the wall of my tent because it was too damn cold to sleep. I had thick wool socks on and black tights under a wool skirt and a cardigan, plus my scarf and mittens. The sleeping bag was Sunshine's, and it was high-tech and built for low temps, and *still,* I was cold to my bones. The snow underneath the tent seeped up and into me like icy fingers pushing at my skin.

I opened my mouth and watched my breath fog in the air.

And then the howling started.

Wolves. Or coyotes. But probably wolves.

They sounded close.

There was a light on in Neely's tent and he was sitting up when I unzipped the front flap and let myself in.

"Hey, Violet," he said, and laughed his low, chuckling laugh. "Was it the cold or the howling?"

"Both," I said back.

"Don't worry. Wolves don't attack people."

I shrugged. "Have you ever read that part in *My Antonia* about Russia, and the bridal party, and the wolves? Maybe we should go sleep in the car."

But Neely just laughed again. He patted the sleeping bag next to him. "Climb in. I wasn't using it anyway. Can't sleep."

He didn't have to offer twice. I slipped off my winter boots and slid into the red bag. Neely had a book beside him, unopened—a wintry book full of orphans and family secrets and misadventures and lies and epic misfortune.

"Read to me?" I asked him.

And he did. Neely had a great voice for reading and soon the wailing of the wild dogs outside bled into the wild winter setting of the book and suddenly I was content and sleepy and doing all right again.

Later he offered me a sip of cognac from a flask to heat me up from the inside, and took one himself too. Then he climbed into the sleeping bag with me. Because it was big enough. And because I wasn't going back to my tent all by myself, no way in hell.

Neely's breath warmed the hollow of my throat, right where the jade-green necklace met my skin, and it felt good.

"Do you think the devil-boy story could be true?" I asked him, because suddenly I felt I had to get the question off my chest, or die trying. "Could it be Brodie up there in the mountains, doing those things? Or River?"

I could feel Neely shrug next to me in the dark. "I don't know. Devil-boy stealing girls' dreams . . . could be them. Both of them. Either. Could be nothing. I guess we'll find out."

I looked up straight into his face, my blue eyes on his. "So you think it could be the both of them, working together?"

River, you wouldn't, would you? Even if you killed the entire town of Rattlesnake Albee, even if you made my uncle slit his own throat, even if you made that kid throw himself in front of a train, you're not evil. Not evil like Brodie. Not deep down. You hated him, just as much as we did.

Didn't you?

"Yes," Neely said, after a minute, in answer to my question.

And then he flipped over to face the other wall of the

tent, as if he didn't want me to keep looking into his eyes.

"Then you think River's gone mad," I said. Statement. Not a question. "You think he went crazy from the glow and teamed up with Brodie, just like Brodie wanted all along."

"Yes. No. I don't know. He's just been gone a long time, is all." And Neely didn't laugh when he said this. He didn't shrug. He was just . . . quiet.

I put my hand on his side, on the soft part between his ribs and his hip. He reached back, grabbed my fingers, and pulled me up next to him, tight.

And if I wished he was River, and if he wished I didn't wish he was River, well, neither of us said anything because he was still warm, and I was still cold, and both of us needed the comfort. Neely-warmth started warming me up, finally, finally, and we both fell asleep wrapped up together with the wolves still lullaby-ing us in the background.

CHAPTER 6

THE APPALACHIAN MOUNTAINS had an air of Echo about them, lots of trees and small towns. There was less snow, only an inch in some places, fluffy and new and unfrozen with brown grass still poking through. And we were grateful because it was steep gravel roads much of the time, and Neely's car was a smooth black luxury thing meant for the city, not circumnavigating mysterious mountain paths on the way to hunting down a stranger-hating village plagued by a devil-boy.

The landscape had stayed roughly the same since we turned away from the sea . . . winter, winter, winter, with barren trees and green pines and wooden fences and open fields full of crows. But we were up higher now, and the sky was bigger. Even the clouds were bigger.

"I'd be inclined to paint this, if I had my tools," Luke said, taking a bite of his cheese and apple sandwich.

We'd stopped to have lunch, and were eating standing up because it was too cold to sit on the ground. Luke was facing a little clearing in the trees. There was an old brown barn in the shape of one of the Citizen's vintage art deco clocks—square on the bottom, dome-shaped above. It stood gazing out at us as we gazed at it, the mountains rising blue in the background.

There hadn't been room in Neely's car for paints and canvases. And I think my brother was missing it, the painting, like how I was already missing my distracted parents, and Jack, and my closet full of Freddie's old clothes, and just about everything I was used to. Being away from home was an eerie thing, thick and powerful and overwhelming. It was energizing to see new places and people, your brain on fire, your heart stirred up. But it was also kind of . . . sad too.

I'd been itching to leave Echo and now that I was on the road, I felt an itchy need to get back home again, damn it. There was no satisfying me.

"You know what this scene needs?" Sunshine stepped in front of the barn, swung her brown hair under her blue hat, and struck a curvy, sultry pose, one palm spread open on her hip. She batted her sleepy eyes at Luke. "Me. That's what."

Luke laughed. "I've already promised to do your portrait when we get back home. How much of my art do you plan to take over?"

Sunshine shrugged, and then turned to me. "A nude," she said, smiling. "I'm going to make him hang it in the Citizen's art gallery ballroom, right next to all those naked paintings of Freddie."

I looked from Sunshine, to my brother, and back again. Then I tilted my head back, clenched my fists, very, very dramatic, and screamed. *"Nooooooo."*

My voice echoed off the silent mountains and came back to me, and Neely started laughing. I pointed at my brother. "If you paint our next-door neighbor in the nude, then you damn well better hide it under your bed, because if I have to look at it I'll kill someone. Probably you."

"I'd love to see that," Neely said, his arms crossed, his back leaning against his now very dirty car.

"Sunshine's nude painting or me killing someone?" I asked.

"Both," Neely said, and then he was laughing that laugh again, his eyes crinkling up with it, and the next thing I knew I was laughing along with him.

Luke tossed an apple core over the fence, into the snow, short and quick and cocky-like. "You're such a prude, Vi."

Sunshine nodded. "It's true, Vi. It's always been true."

I opened my mouth. Closed it. Opened it again. "Would a prude do what I did with River? Would she? Even after he suicided Jack's Pa, even after all of it? Would she have let him do what he almost did?" And then I shut my mouth again, seeing the looks on their faces.

Especially Neely's.

His eyes had changed. They'd been happy and amused half a second ago. And now they were hot and dark and fiery.

"You were under his glow, Vi," he said, the blush spilling off his face and spreading down his neck like it did sometimes right before he let his fists start swinging. "That wasn't your fault."

"Wasn't it?" I asked, but my voice barely rose above the cold breeze blowing down the mountains.

Wasn't it, River?

≈

We found Inn's End just as the sun started sinking into the horizon. We pulled over no less than eight times, asking farmers and postmen and kids playing in the snow for directions. It wasn't on the maps, just as Wide-Eyed Theo had said.

Everyone gave us directions willingly enough, though they looked at us strangely and seemed a bit unnerved at the question. Even the kids—a brother and sister on a small farm, wrapped up against the chill. They were no older than ten, with grave expressions, like old black-and-white pictures of towheaded Great Depression children I'd seen in *National Geographic*. They came up to Neely's rolled-down car window and the green-eyed older brother peered over the top of the car door and told us where to go . . . down this road, up the next, very earnest, as if he were being graded on it. And when he was done he rubbed a calloused un-mittened hand over a small cut on his left temple.

I wondered what work he'd been doing at his age, to get hands like that. I wondered how he'd gotten the cut on his face.

The boy caught my eye and added, "You shouldn't go there, though. Bad things happen in Inn's End. It's a bad place." And his little sister pursed up her chapped red lips and nodded too, like it was the God-given truth, praise be to him.

But it would take more than two wary little kids to make us turn back now, even if the directions were full of wrong turns and dead ends and misleads, as if people didn't want us to find the town. Two hours it took us. Two hours of twisting roads and black trees and dark hollows. And then we turned down another unnamed, unpaved road, crossed a covered bridge, and there we were.

The town sign was weathered and tilted at an angle, but we could still read it.

Inn's End.

I guess I had built it up in my mind as a wild backwoods place with barefoot children and chickens running around squawking and rusted-out washtubs and weathered, beaten-down shacks. The reality was a windy, one-main-street town with a vague New England feel that reminded me of Echo, just like the rest of the Appalachian Mountains. The white wooden houses looked suspicious and tight-lipped, with their black shutters closed tight against the wind, but the outskirts of the town backed up into sloping meadows, which themselves backed up into endless rolling hills and trees, trees, trees. Beautiful.

We parked the car next to the small, steepled, red-roofed church at the end of the main road. We got out. Stood still. Took the town in.

The first thing I noticed was the quiet. The deep, deep, middle-of-the-forest quiet. After the quiet, I noticed the lack of Christmas decorations. No lights on trees, no greenery around door frames, no cheery red tinsel hung between streetlights. All the towns we'd passed recently had put up their own slightly shabby holiday trimmings, making the streets seem more cheerful and sweet than usual. But not Inn's End.

And then I noticed the birds.

Black-feathered corpses. Everywhere. Piled up on steps, kicked into snow piles, dangling by their necks from lampposts and signs. There were eight nailed to the door of the dark, abandoned-looking Youngman's Inn, and five hanging by their feet from the iron church gate.

The four of us walked down the center of the road. Still and silent. I saw lights in windows, but there was no one in the street. Not a soul.

The sun was just a sliver on the horizon now, like a small prayer said without much hope. The orange-pink light reflected off the snow and turned the world a strange, ominous color that put dark thoughts in my head.

"What was it that Wide-Eyed Theo said?" Neely asked, quiet.

"The devil-boy commands a flock of ravens," Luke said, voice low.

I shivered, a sick, hard shiver, like the ones you get when you have the flu.

My wrists started hurting, sharp and cold at first, and then hot and full of sting. I tore my mittens off and turned my hands over, but all I saw was the same pink scars, looking like they always did.

"I don't like it here," Luke said. His words fogged up in the cold air. His eyes were wide open, his arms straight down at his sides. "Vi, I have a bad feeling about this town. This—" He nodded his chin at the dead birds, their feathers ruffling in the chill wind. "I don't like it, sister. We should leave. Now."

Sunshine turned around in a circle, saying nothing. So far she and Luke had flirted and kissed and been in love and acting like this trip was all good fun.

But now I saw it in her eyes. Fear. Raw and rotten and deep as winter is cold.

A door opened. One of the white houses at the far end of the street. It opened and then slammed closed again. The attached cluster of dead, black feathers swung back with it and hit the wood with a thud.

A girl stood on the steps.

She saw us just as we saw her. She jumped back a few inches, her mouth wide open.

Two heartbeats.

And then she started walking toward us, her eyes on Luke and his red-brown hair.

"Who are you?" she asked, her voice small and hesitant like it was afraid to be heard. "Where did you come from? We don't get strangers here." She paused. "At least, we didn't use to."

I thought she was about fourteen, but slight and small, which might be making her look younger. She had white-blond hair, straight down her back, no bangs. She wore a green dress, a bit old-fashioned in a home-sewn way, plain with a tight waist, thick black boots, and a gray homemade sweater—one thread was coming loose and had opened a quarter-sized hole on her shoulder. In her right arm she held a large white bowl of something. Something thick and red that had sloshed over the side and stained the front of her dress.

She was looking at Luke but Neely answered her. "We heard about your town, about what was happening here. The devil-boy, with the ravens. We came to investigate."

"No, Neely, don't tell her," I whispered, too late. I'd read mysteries. I'd read Agatha Christie. You never tell people what you're up to. It's the golden rule. If people know you're looking for answers, they clam up and refuse to talk.

But Neely just winked at me, and then at her, as if we were all just a bunch of kids flirting with each other at the town carnival or something, our hands sticky from cotton candy and our hearts on our sleeves.

How did he do that? Make a hidden mountain town full of dead birds feel like a Norman Rockwell painting?

The girl nodded, as if what Neely said made sense and nothing could surprise her much anymore anyway.

"What's in the bowl?" Sunshine had a hand to her

mouth, and suddenly I knew why. The winter wind lifted the copper smell to my nose.

"Blood," the girl said, simply. "For the churchyard. We killed the pig today."

Luke turned his head to look back at the church, then turned it forward again. "Why are you bringing pig's blood to the church?"

His voice got loud at the end, and it worried me. I wrapped my fingers around his arm and he leaned into me.

The girl shrugged. "To pour on the gravestones."

"Why would you pour pig's blood on the gravestones?" I didn't really want to know the answer, and yet the question came out of my mouth anyway.

The girl shifted her hip and put the bowl in her other arm, more of it spilling onto her dress in the process.

A sound came from Sunshine's opened lips. A . . . sigh. A soft sigh. Usually Sunshine shrieked loudly when she was scared, or pretending to be scared. But she was quiet now. Sighs, not screams.

The girl looked at Sunshine, and then looked back at the blood staining her home-sewn dress. A flush started creeping over her cheeks, as if she hadn't thought to be embarrassed about the spilled blood before now.

"It's an offering to our ancestors, to help capture the boy," she said, in answer to my question. The girl paused, looked toward her house, quick, and then looked back at us again. "Some people are saying he's the devil and has hooves for feet and fire coming out of his fingertips, but it's wrong. It's all wrong. He . . . he just looks like a boy, just a boy like either of you." She stopped and stared at Neely, and then at Luke. "I saw him when he came to me, in my bedroom. He sat on my stomach, light as air, and tried to steal my dreams, only I woke up. The other girls, they didn't wake up in time, they didn't see his face in the dark, but I struck a match. I saw."

Neely flinched when the girl said *a boy, just a boy like either of you.*

The girl started blinking fast, and her eyes were pleading and wistful and kind of lonely. That look was familiar to me, in some deep, almost forgotten way.

"I didn't tell anyone," she said. "The other girls told, but I didn't."

I wanted to ask her more, and so did Neely, behind me. His mouth was parted and I could almost see his questions, sitting on the edge of his tongue . . .

But I felt so bad for her suddenly, with her red-rimmed eyes and her skinny shoulders all hunched up and the blood on her dress. I didn't care about anything, right then. Not the devil-boy, not the dead birds, not Brodie. There was just this girl.

I pulled myself away from Luke, and stepped forward. "Let's go to the cemetery and get this done, okay?" I nodded at the bowl, and then I reached for her free hand. It was small and calloused, like the boy who gave us directions. I took it in mine, and squeezed.

We all walked back down the road, past all the white houses with the tight black shutters and the dead birds on the doors, to the church. I opened the black iron gate, careful not to touch the birds, not to look into their black eyes, and pulled the girl in behind me.

"My name is Pine," she said as we climbed up to the tiny cemetery off to the left of the church. "Like the trees. My mother likes the way they smell. And how they never die, even in winter."

"I'm Violet," I said. "And that's Luke, my twin brother, and our next-door neighbor Sunshine, and our friend Neely."

She looked at them in turn, and nodded. The cemetery was on a small hill, the gravestones leaning and crouching and huddled together. I glanced down the horizon. From up here the mountains seemed to be nestling the whole town in the crook of its arm.

Pine stepped up to the nearest gravestone, the sky behind her a dusky blue, edged in a scorching red-orange. She lifted the bowl and poured about a quarter cup of the blood right over the top. *"And thou shalt slay the swine, and thou shalt take its blood, and sprinkle it on the stones,"* she said, soft and slow, like a prayer.

It was getting dark, fast, but I could still see the stains of previous offerings, turning the worn, crooked stone an unsettling color, flaking off onto the ground like shavings of rust.

"Why do you do this?" I asked, moving with her over to the next stone, a tall one. I helped her lift the lip of the bowl and dribble the blood over the letters, GRIEVE, until they were coated. There were no other words carved on it, just Grieve.

She shrugged again, a tight moving up and down of her shoulders. "Because we always have. Whenever someone has a baby that's sick, or an Elderly that needs to move on, or a kid gone missing in the woods, we make a blood offering to our ancestors."

We moved on down the line. Neely and Luke and Sunshine stood about fifteen yards away, watching from the edge of the cemetery at the base of the hill, not talking. Both Luke and Sunshine clutched the iron gate in their fists, like they couldn't wait to leave.

Three days ago we were singing Christmas songs in Citizen Kane, and now I was helping a sad girl in a dead-bird town pour blood in a churchyard. Life was . . . strange.

It was the last headstone, number nineteen, and we were down to the drops. I vaguely wished in the back of my mind for a spatula, something to scrape the last bits out of the bowl, like Freddie had done when we made Dutch Coffee Chocolate Cake.

And then I shivered. Shivered at the absurdity of scraping pig's blood from a bowl like cake batter. My shivering arms splattered the last red beads on the ground instead of the stone, and they made small, melted dents in the snow. Four little black holes.

This town was too quiet.

Too . . . *bizarre.*

Something was wrong. Off. Something worse than dead birds and blood.

I could feel the bowl in my hands, see the dead birds, hear the sound of my feet crunching on snow. It was real.

Wasn't it?

River, am I being glowed?

Or sparked?

Are we all?

I shook my head. Blinked.

River's glow felt good.

And Brodie's spark hurt like hell.

I would know. I felt sure I would know.

Pine took the bowl from me and set it on the ground.

She stood up, and shuddered as the cold wind hit her small body. I took the scarf from around my neck, my new striped one, and wrapped it around her, moving her white-blond hair as I did it. "Keep this," I said. "I've got another back home."

"People will ask where it came from," she said, not taking her eyes from the pretty white and black stripes.

"Just tell them you found it in the forest," I replied.

She looked up at me. "Thank you."

I stared into her light blue-gray eyes. "Pine, are all your ancestors buried here, in this graveyard? It's so small . . ."

She nodded. "A group of them came over from Scotland, way, way back when. Married each other. We . . . keep to ourselves." She tilted her chin up, like she was ready for my scorn. "We used to go to a real school down the mountain, but Pastor Walker Rose stopped that. Now we go to school in the church right there, three days a week. Duncan Begg and his daughter Prudence teach us, ever since Widow McGregor died. It's mostly knitting and carving and carpentry, but they do reading and math too."

"Pine, what do all the dead birds on the signs and doors mean? Does this have something to do with the devil-boy?"

She looked up at me, again. I wasn't that tall, but she was still a good six inches smaller. "The Droods, they caught the boy in their daughter's room. They tried to stop him, get him off Charlotte, but a flock of ravens swept in through the window and started pecking at their eyes and face and head and hands. They still have the sores. The herb woman says they're not healing clean." She paused. "And then there's all the people, mostly older but some children too, who say they've seen him in the woods, dressed all in black, with a dark cloud of ravens flying above him, following him wherever he goes."

I could picture him, clear as day. Brodie. Red hair. Midnight-blue sky. White snow. Black ravens.

Neely had joined me by this time, stepping up beside me, listening quietly. Luke and Sunshine still hovered by the iron gate, whispering to each other.

"So these Droods still have the sores?" Neely. "Then the birds aren't an illusion. It means he's controlling animals now too. That can't be good." The grin was back on Neely's face like it was nothing, like it was just a bit of juicy gossip, like it was, *For what do we live but to make sport for our neighbors and laugh at them in our turn.*

"They think killing the birds will anger him," Pine added. "Make him come out into the open so we can catch him. But he's gone. I know he is. I can feel it, in my insides, somehow. A . . . lessening. Ma made me bring the blood out here, to ask our ancestors for help. But I know he's already gone."

Neely's eyes had that up-to-no-good glint that I'd seen in River's so many times. And that's when I knew we were going to stay.

And maybe part of me was scared, but the other part, the louder part . . . the Freddie part . . . was licking its lips in anticipation.

"Pine, do you know somewhere we can spend the night?" I looked up and down the small rows of houses that led off the main street, and her gaze followed mine. "A campground, maybe? Or a hotel?"

Pine shook her head, snuggling her chin into the scarf. "We had an inn once, a long, long time ago. A road ran through Inn's End, and a train too. We were the last stop before the big forest. But then Pastor Walker Rose started preaching against strangers. Soon the train disappeared and then no more inn either." She was quiet for a moment. "You could stay at the Lashleys', I suppose. Their place is on the other edge of town. It's the biggest house in Inn's End—the one with the rope swing in front."

"Do they rent out rooms?" I asked, with no enthusiasm. I liked Pine on sight, but the thought of sleeping in one of the houses in Inn's End, with the dead birds hanging on the door . . .

But Pine shook her head. "No one rents out rooms here. Not since Walker Rose. The Lashleys . . . they had a little boy. He was really pretty, great brown curls, fat rosy cheeks. Everyone loved him. And then one morning he wandered into the woods and didn't come back. They found him three days later, smashed to pieces at the bottom of a gorge. Little Hamish Lashley's ma threw herself off old Witch William's bridge. They told Ian not to marry an outsider, and a city girl at that, despite the money. But he would have her. He ran off then too. Who knows where, anywhere that's not here, I guess. No one lives there now. It's empty."

A raven cawed from overhead. I looked up. It was perched on the steeple roof, sitting with its chest puffed out as if to say *I'm not dead like the others. Not yet.*

"That will work for the night," I said to Pine. "Thank you. Will people mind, though?" I added, as I saw an old bent woman step out of a small, dark shop with three dead birds on the door and no sign. She shuffled down the street and disappeared into the night, never turning her head, not seeing us.

Pine just shrugged again.

"Well, that's comforting," Neely said, and grinned.

≈

We hid our car back by the covered Witch William's bridge, parking it into the trees a bit so the shadows would help hide it come daybreak. Just in case. Just until we knew what morning would bring. We grabbed sleeping bags, toothbrushes, clothes, and the picnic basket, and then headed back into town.

The Lashley house was beautiful. Even with the dirty windows, and the overgrown shrubs almost covering the steps and door. The neglect, the decay . . . it felt like the Citizen. It felt like home.

We stood in the dark, under the moon, watching the rope swing move this way and that in the frigid night wind. I could almost see the Lashley boy, curls and cheeks, sitting on it and laughing.

"Well, I guess this is where we sleep tonight," Neely said, taking in the house and smiling. "Should be memorable."

"No." Luke stood at the edge of the lawn, shaking his head. "Vi, I can't do it. We can't stay here. We'll never be able to fall asleep, it's not safe, they don't want us here—that girl said so. What kind of town pours blood on gravestones? They'll come for us in the night, sis, they will, I just know it . . ."

Sunshine clutched her sleeping bag in her arms. "Luke's right. This town is stupid and this house is stupid. And we'll be stupid if we stay here."

I could have teased them about being scared. They would have done it in my shoes.

"It's just for one night," I said. "Where are we going to go this late? Inn's End is miles from a main road, and we'll never be able to find our way back here again. We barely found it the first time. Besides, think of the great story this will make. Think of the great art it will inspire, brother."

Luke stared at me for a second, and then shrugged. But I could still see it in his eyes, the anxiety. He looked at Sunshine, and then back at the town behind him, his muscles tensed, like he was trying to suppress a shiver.

I set down the picnic basket, crossed my arms over my chest, and hugged myself tight. Luke's unease was getting to me. This silent, forgotten town . . . the dead birds . . . that blood . . .

Still. I wasn't going to run. I'd wanted this, after all.

"Vi's right, Luke," Neely said, his Neely glint still flashing in his blue Neely eyes. "This should be a night to remember."

And he walked up the steps of the abandoned house, laughing.

CHAPTER 7

November

We found a secret passageway one night. A hidden door in the large storage room off the Glenship's main kitchen. Chase stumbled upon the hidden latch while reading French poetry out loud to a pretty maid while she hid from the housekeeper.

Will laughed out loud when he saw it open, the brick wall separating like a row of teeth opening to take a bite. "Atta boy, Chase," he said. "Atta boy."

We followed the hallway as it grew colder and darker, colder and darker. It went on and on. We finally turned up underneath a trapdoor in the conservatory in the Glenship's large, manicured garden. We climbed the ladder and popped out like characters on a moonlit stage. The warm humidity was exotic and sensuous after the cold tunnel, and I breathed in deep.

"So that's how they're getting the hooch in and out," Chase said. "The back road leads right up to the greenhouse here. I should have guessed. All that noise in the middle of the night . . ."

And suddenly I realized there was more to Chase's father, and their money, than I'd thought. Chase held a flask to my lips, and the gin singed my insides, just like that first time, in the wine cellar, when it mixed up with Will's burn and clouded the world and led us into sin. Gin would always taste like fire and Will and sin, to me.

When the flask was gone, and we were drunk on it, and on the heady smell of the flowers, and the thick greenhouse air, we collapsed in a heap in a corner. A large green fern tickled us with its tickly fern leaves every time we moved, and it made us laugh and laugh.

Will took our hands, both Chase's and mine, and made the stars twinkling above the glass roof glow, glow so bright they were no longer stars, but pebbled-sized suns. And then he made them dance. And form themselves into the letters of our names.

And the next day Chase thought it had just been the drunk in him, but I knew all along, didn't I.

≈≈≈

The boys gathered twigs and branches from the snowy backyard and Sunshine started a fire in the fireplace. I warned everyone about sooty chimneys and how they made you fall over dead. But no one listened because it was freezing.

It was long past twilight. I sat down on the floor in front of the fire. My skin warmed in the heat and my hair glowed orange in its light. I wanted to keep reading Freddie's diary, and thinking about Will Redding and his burn, and River Redding and his glow, and let the thrill and fear of it all fill me up until I started liking it.

But not now. Later. When I could be alone. And when I wasn't sitting in an abandoned house in a forgotten town that hated devils and ravens and strangers.

The door to the Lashley house had been unlocked—I guess theft wasn't a concern here, just like it wasn't in Echo. Inside, it had been untouched, stopped in time, like Miss Havisham in her wedding dress with the clock and the cake. Wooden toys, furry from dust, cluttered the high-ceiling sitting room, lying just where they'd been left. Flowered wallpaper surrounded Victorian furniture—the stiff, high-backed chairs and sofas, the fringed lampshades, the elaborately framed mirror above the fireplace.

We explored everything the moment we got inside. Everything but the attic, which was locked, and the cellar, which was pitch-black and full of grisly, scurrying night sounds. We'd forgotten the flashlights in the car, so the search was done in icy semi-darkness, lit only with a candle Neely found in the kitchen. The master bedroom was large and neat. A satin caramel-colored nightdress hung on a hook in the bathroom, and small, feminine glass bottles and jars were still arranged tidily in front of the mirror. Everything was stiff with cold, especially the bed cover and the curtains. I ran my hand down rigid silk and dust flew.

The nursery. Sunshine opened the door, but none of us went in. Boy things, everywhere, shoes and toys and books and a rocking horse and . . .

. . . And all I could think about was a small crushed boy body, tangled in leaves and shadows.

I knew what it would have looked like. I knew, more than most.

Neely came over to me by the fire, moka pot in hand.

Yes, we'd brought the little silver espresso maker with us. He set it near the flames, and soon I heard a low, hot-water sound. The familiar dark coffee smell burst through the room, sweeping away the thick smell of dust and neglect.

We all sipped the joe for a while, sitting on our sleeping bags in front of the fire. We wouldn't be sleeping in the beds. No way we would be sleeping in the beds. And we wanted to all be together, anyway. Maybe nothing would happen. Maybe everything would be quiet, and we would wake to warm sunshine and spend the day questioning the town about the devil-boy and then go on our merry way.

But I doubted it. And everyone else did too, judging by the way Luke and Sunshine had forgotten to be in love with each other, and the way Sunshine jumped at every sound, and the way Neely kept getting up to stare out the big Victorian windows into the night outside, and the way Luke never let me out of sight for more than three seconds.

Still, despite all this, I felt bustling, energized, fired up. Even if this town scared the damn hell out of me. Even if Brodie could be out there, right now, his tall, thin body weaving between dead trees, his red hair looking black in the dark, his birds flying behind him like a damn ebony cloak.

I pulled red logs of spicy chorizo out of the basket, and we roasted them on the fire. Oil dripped into the flames and made them hum. We had more of Neely's coffee and four crisp apples and a wedge of nutty Dutch cheese.

For dessert Neely gathered fresh clean snow in a glass bowl from the square kitchen. He opened a jar of maple syrup he found in the cupboard, and drizzled it on top. We all ate from the same dish, using big silver spoons, the fluffy white melting away to smooth, earthy sweetness on our tongues.

When we were done, Luke and Sunshine washed the bowl and spoons with more clean snow, since there was no running water in the house. They dried the dishes, and put them back in the kitchen, like we lived in this damn house now.

Luke and Sunshine fell asleep in minutes, despite Luke's earlier protest. I drifted off in front of the fire eventually, coming in and out of consciousness, small sounds waking me with a jerk, my dreams tense and twisted. And each time I awoke . . . there was Neely. Not sleeping. Pacing. Watching.

He woke us at midnight.

Neely had found a radio buried in a closet upstairs when we searched the house. I hadn't been able to bring myself to touch the woman's dresses, so small and bright and . . . unused. So it was Neely who pushed through the clothes of the dead woman, to the back, to the shelf where he found the radio.

Luke, Sunshine, and I rubbed sleep from our eyes, sat up, and then shivered as our shoulders hit the cold. We moved our sleeping bags even closer together, and Neely threw another thick branch on the fire.

He started fiddling with the dials, but Luke just stared at the radio and shook his head. "I'm not listening to that show again. Not here, in this creepy house in this creepy town. I won't do it."

Sunshine was glaring at the radio too. "That stupid radio show is the reason we're sitting here in this cold house in this nightmarish town, instead of drinking hot chocolate in the Citizen. Wide-Eyed Theo can go to hell."

"Shut up, you cowards," I said, because, damn it, I wanted to listen to Theo, so help me God. I owed it to him. Without Theo, I would still be home, staring at the sea, about ready to scream at the silence and the boredom and the waiting, waiting, waiting . . .

Neely looked from Luke, to Sunshine, to me, and smiled. He spun the left knob—

. . . of the mad and true. It's Wide-Eyed Theo. I'm here. You're here. And it's the witching hour. Time for your daily dose of Stranger Than Fiction.

Neely sat down next to me and cuddled up close in the cold.

So . . . anyone out there find Inn's End? Any reports on the devil-boy and the ravens? Please call in. 1-800-EYE-THEO. Keep Theo in the loop, kids.

I did hear back from one brave, loyal follower. Jason H. called in from, quote, "an ominously quiet corner of Washington State" to report on that kid who claimed he was talking to a dead boy in his attic. This ghost told him to start digging a four-foot-by-four-foot hole in his backyard . . . and the boy eventually dug up the remains of a small child. Police are looking into it. Thanks for the closure, Jason. A Wide-Eyed Theo Kit is coming your way, complete with an EMF meter and apocalypse-ready hand-crank radio.

I have three new stories tonight for you greedy little bastards. This first one comes out of Maine, a town named Riddle. Two young sisters are claiming that a teenage boy is living in an old, unused barn buried in the woods behind the sisters' farm. The boy only comes out at night, and disappears whenever anyone but the sisters are near. The girls have been leaving him apples and chocolate. But now the boy wants the sisters to come into the barn to, quote, "see something they will find meaningful."

They want to know if they should follow this boy into the barn. Well, believers? What do you think?

My other two stories both come out of North Carolina.

Apparently the residents of some small island off the North Carolina coast have started a sea god cult. They worship a boy who commands the ocean and demands virgin sacrifices to appease his violent appetite.

Take that as you will, believers. My source called in late last night—she seemed confused and possibly drunk. She lost track of what she was saying by the end of our conversation, and didn't remember who I was, or why she had called in the first place, so I didn't get the name of the island. But if any of you listeners find it, well, do let me know. All I could get out of her was "Wild Horses," whatever that means. Could be the name of a hotel . . . or the name of a beach. Not sure, not sure.

My last story, as I said, is also out of North Carolina, though I didn't catch where before the caller hung up. It involves a haunted fisherman's shack. Teenagers go in and don't come out again. That's all the details I have. And if this sounds like pure urban legend, then perhaps it is. But it is our job to believe, and so we must.

It's Wide-Eyed Theo, signing off for the night.

Go forth and find the strange.

"Riddle," Luke said, staring straight at me. "That's only thirty miles from Echo."

"I know," I replied. Riddle was a village nestled in the deep Maine woods like something from a German fairy tale. Freddie had taken us there once, when we were little.

She met a young man in the forest at the edge of town and disappeared with him into the trees, leaving Luke and me just standing there, staring into the dark. When she came back, some ten minutes later, she was pale, but cheerful. I never did solve that Freddie mystery. It was just one of the many.

"I don't like it," I added. "I don't like that Theo mentioned a town so close to the Citizen."

Luke nodded. Sunshine nodded. Neely laughed.

"Looks like our devil-boy has moved on, as that Pine girl said. The only question is . . ." Neely leaned back against the flowered wall by the big front window and smiled one of his careless smiles. "Which way did he go?"

I opened my mouth to answer . . .

And then I saw the lights, flashing in the dark outside.

"They're here," I said, and my voice was calm, strangely calm, like I had known all along what was going to happen.

I heard Luke climb out of his sleeping bag. Felt his hand grip my arm, hard. Sunshine grabbed a thick marble candlestick from the mantel above the fireplace, and held it at her side, fist clenched like she was ready for it . . . but then her free hand went to her head, cradling it in the spot where the baseball bat hit it last summer. She dropped the candlestick on the ground and it thudded, deep. She backed into a corner of the room and crouched in the shadows, her long hair covering the white of her face.

But Neely just kept standing at the window, shaking his head.

"It's not what you think," he said. And then he opened the door.

CHAPTER 8

TORCH LIGHTS.

We stood out on the front step, watching, not caring who saw us now.

Twenty or so men walked down the street outside the house. There were dogs at their heels and they were carrying torches, *torches,* like they'd been out hunting monsters. Twenty men and a swarm of dogs and one boy, tied up and held tight and dragged between them.

The men were quiet, making no sound but the crunch-crunch of boots on snow. Their torches shifted slightly with each step, and long shadows slithered and danced across the trees and houses.

The boy was slack, the firelight flashing off his long hair as it swung about his ears.

Long, red hair.

"It's him, it's Brodie," Sunshine said in a hollow, quiet voice, her eyes staring straight out, her body stiff and still except for the palm she still held to her head.

I took her free hand and squeezed. Luke stayed hunched in the doorway behind me, and whispered *we need to get out of here, Vi,* over and over.

People were coming out of their houses now, children in socks and women in white nightdresses under black woolen coats grabbed from a peg by the door. The children cheered at the sight of the red-haired boy, their arms raised. But the mothers . . . the mothers put their hands together under their chins, or one palm on their heart, and stayed as silent as the men.

The four of us were out on the street now, our socks getting soaked up with snow. We watched the men march the boy up into the squat, white church, to the Gothic-arch-framed doorway. They pulled back the two heavy wooden doors and went inside.

The church bell started ringing a minute later, urgent and crisp.

Back inside the Lashley house.

Neely said nothing and his cheeks turned red and his eyes went dark.

"What are we going to do?" I asked, because no one

had. "We can't control Brodie. He almost killed us the last time. We should have talked about this. What the hell is our plan, Neely?"

Neely started moving a bit, side to side, like he was eager and it was getting hard to stand still. "Don't worry, Vi. He's already captured. The town did us a favor. They caught him. I don't know how, but they caught him. Maybe he over-sparked himself and went weak from it. Maybe they have their own magic here. I don't know." His hands were twitching. I could see them. "But we'll go to the church. We'll see what they plan to do."

Neely was right. Brodie was caught, captured, tied up. River wasn't here, he was safe somewhere, laying low, as he'd promised. It was just Brodie. Had been all along. Everything led up to this. Everything since Brodie cut my wrists and kissed me, everything since I'd stabbed him in the chest and passed out. One step after another, all leading to this.

Finding Brodie.

Getting vengeance.

Watching him die.

The bat, and Sunshine bleeding, and strips of red across Jack's skin, River, blood on his neck, and the waiting, and the dark corners and shadows and hearing laughter that wasn't there, and it will never ever end, ever. Ever. Unless.

I was fidgeting too now, all fear gone, nothing but courage beating in my blood. I shoved my feet into my winter boots, quick, quick, and the tune popped back into my head, the one from the beach, the one that went *A-hunting I will go, a-hunting I will go . . .*

"No."

I turned. Luke. His hand shot out and gripped my arm again.

"No," he said. "I won't let you. Let's just leave, Vi, okay? Let's just get out of here, leave the sleeping bags, leave everything, and just get to the car. Now."

I put my hand on his, and then gently, gently, pulled his fingers away. "I have to go, Luke. I have to. This is it. If they kill Brodie, I need to be there. I need to be sure it's him. And I'll need to be sure he's . . ." I paused. "I'll need to be sure he's dead."

Luke met my eyes. And nodded. Once.

"You should pack up while we're gone," I said to him, in a louder voice. "Sunshine, you stay and help him. When this is done, we'll meet you at the car and then we'll leave Inn's End and never look back, all right?"

And I was out the door before my brother could say another word, Neely right behind me.

I expected the hard stares but I wasn't prepared for them. The looks from the Inn's End residents as we walked up the church steps . . . they cut sharper than the winter wind that blew right through me.

No one stopped us, though.

The church was already almost full. The only light came from the fat candles that sat on the windowsills lining the wall. Shadows crept and crawled across the stark, stark room, nothing to see but a stained-glass window depicting a pink beast, lying on its back, legs raised in the air, neck spilling blood. The stiff wooden pews were packed with families huddled and bundled up in the great, white, unheated room. It smelled like apples and snow and candles and wet wool. Neely and I squeezed into the last bench on the left, deep in the shadows, next to an elderly couple who refused to look us in the eye. Neely's elbow brushed by the woman, and she cringed against her husband.

The boy was by the pulpit, half hidden by the group of men. He just stood there, alone, his chin on his chest. Tangled red hair covered his face, hiding his features, and his arms were twisted behind him and tied. He wore black wool slacks and a hand-knit sweater like Pine's. His clothes were torn in places, his pale, bare skin showing through. Dead leaves and twigs and dirt clung to every inch of him, as if he'd been living in the wild for years, running with wolves and sleeping in trees.

I felt bad for him. I did. Even if it was Brodie. Even knowing it was probably Brodie. I still flinched at the sight of him, alone and tied up and waiting for whatever horrible thing was going to happen next.

The candlelight rippled over his body in flickering bursts. I strained forward.

"Is it him?" I whispered to Neely. I pressed on my wrists. They had started hurting again. "It can't be him, though. Look how he's standing. Brodie would never stand like that, so quiet and patient and doomed."

Neely kept staring at the boy. "River was here. Or Brodie. One of them, I'm almost sure of it. But—" He just shook his head, and kept staring.

I saw Pine's white-blond hair shining from one of the front rows. She was still wearing the scarf I gave her. There were six children next to her and an older woman that I figured must be her mother, though she looked close to sixty. I wanted Pine to turn. I wanted to see her face, to see what she was thinking about the captured boy. But she didn't look back.

A man stepped away from the torch-carrying group and came to stand at the front of the aisle between the two rows of pews. His shoulders were strong and wide, his pale blue eyes big and piercing and grim, not a drop of mischief or humor. His beard was thick, and soft-looking, and brown turning to gray.

"And so," he said, his voice booming across the room, rock solid and deep, "we have finally caught the devil that plagued our daughters these past weeks. I don't need to tell you the horror I felt the night I heard a noise and walked into Prue's room, just in time to see a flash of red hair slipping out the window, a string of black birds trailing behind."

People began to talk, loudly, all at once, telling their own stories of the devil-boy and his birds. The voices bounced off the rafters and echoed off the white walls and the room swelled with sound. The bearded man waited a few seconds, then held up his hand.

"The question is," he said, "what to do with him? There is no precedent for devils. Witches, yes, as you know. That is simple. Our ancestors took care of them years ago. And thanks to Pastor Walker Rose, God rest his soul, we haven't had any since my father was young. But devils . . . this is a delicate matter, not to be rushed. Drood there wants to hang him—"

Here he nodded at another man, a man with a bandage over his eye and several seeping sores on his face.

"But," the bearded man said, "as I told Drood, a hanging may not kill a devil. Burning has been suggested, though that, in my mind, is for witches and witches alone. Giver

Crisp advised tipping him upside down and draining all the blood from him, as that is what we do to pigs—the idea being that devils and pigs are in the same category, so to speak. I am now opening the floor to other suggestions. Remember, whatever we do, it must be quick. And quiet."

Everyone was silent again. They seemed to be . . . waiting. Their expressions were obedient, but impatient and . . . eager, almost like children trying hard to be still at the end of a long day of school.

I'd seen that eager look before.

River . . . eyes dancing . . . jaw clenched tight . . . right before Jack's dad slit his own throat in Echo's town square . . .

And then I realized, fully, what we'd walked in on. This town, these people . . . it was off. It was all *off*. What had Neely and I been thinking, marching right into the church like we belonged? This town was . . . *wrong*.

"We will do this civilized," the man continued, looking back at the congregation again. "You will raise your hands. Yes, Minnie Brown, go ahead—"

"Duncan. Duncan Begg."

The voice was hoarse, and young, and yet still it soared above the rest of the noise in the church. It came from the red-haired boy. He had . . . changed. He stood straight now, chin up, his hair thrown back. His skin was clear, his forehead wide, his cheeks pink with that healthy glow people sometimes get from spending a lot of time outside.

He looked right at me. Me, and then Neely, right at us, and his eyes were hurt, and dark, and scared, and sane.

Neely's hands, on my own, holding tight, tight, tight. "It's not Brodie," he said, quiet, his mouth near my ear. "It's not Brodie," he said again.

And he was right. How could we have thought it was Brodie? The kid in front of us had the red hair but he was strong and young-Gene-Kelly, not tall, all-elbows-and-knees Texas cowboy.

"Then who is it?" I whispered back. But Neely just kept staring ahead, alert, focused.

"Duncan Begg, you've known me my whole life," the boy called out as the room went pin-drop still. "You taught me how to carve a horse from a piece of white pine when I was five years old. You built my grandmother a special rocking chair to save her back in those hard years before she died. How can you stand there and say I'm this devil-boy?"

The woman on Neely's left, the one who had cringed away from him, made a small noise. She unwound herself from her husband's arms, and stood.

Everyone turned to look at her, and I flinched back farther into the shadows.

"That is Finch Grieve, from out near Sin Hill," the

woman said. "His grandmother and me used to knit the souls of the dead together on Sundays, before her aches and pains stopped her from coming into town. He's not the devil-boy, Duncan. Couldn't be him there."

Finch turned his head, and rested his gaze on her, as did the rest of the crowd.

"You're saying we have the wrong boy?" Duncan's blue eyes were very, very calm. "This is serious, Aggie Lennox. Be sure of your next words. If you are wrong, the people here won't be kind. Revenge is owed." He motioned to Finch. "He has the red hair, flaming red, underneath all that dirt. We found him hiding in the woods, and who hides but the guilty?"

Aggie reached a hand behind her back. Her husband took it in his own, quick, and squeezed. "It's Finch. It's just Finch. He's quiet, always been quiet, and lonely now, I should think, with his mother gone and his grannie too, living all those miles out there on his own. Some would say he has a bit of the moon in him. But that doesn't make him a devil."

Duncan nodded. Slow. "Do you stand by your words, Aggie?"

A pause. Everyone looked at her, even Finch. Especially Finch.

"I stand by my words," she said, loud and clear. And

then she sat back down, next to her husband, and leaned against him.

Her husband looked worried. I saw it in his faded green eyes when they caught mine, before he turned away.

Duncan gazed out over the congregation. He was reading their faces, judging their response. A hand rose. He nodded. "Yes, Didi."

A girl got to her feet. She was ten, maybe eleven, with thick, curly red hair flying out from her head. "The devil can hide in any man," she said. She turned, and looked at Aggie, and at us, and there was a look in her eyes that was not child-like, not innocent.

"The devil can hide in any man," she repeated. "Or any boy. Isn't that so? How do we know whether or not Finch Grieve is still as he once was? Couldn't the devil look like Finch, if he chose? Couldn't he look like anyone?"

A rumbling waved through the crowd, a rumbling of "true, true, out of the mouths of babes, true, true, true."

Another hand in the air. Another nod.

"What if we buried him alive? Put him back under the earth where he came from?"

A dozen more hands raised.

"I think we should bleed him dry, like the pigs. Pour his blood on the gravestones and—"

"No, burning is the only way to know—"

"You got to drown the devil out—we could tie him down with rocks and throw him in Silky Pond."

It was as if Aggie had never spoken.

I shifted in my seat. My breath quickened.

"Don't," Neely said, knowing what I was going to do before I knew it myself. "Don't, Vi—"

I was already on my feet. "It's not him," I cried out. My voice hit the tall angled ceiling and echoed around the church. "We came to Inn's End tonight because we heard the devil-boy was here. He tried to kill me. He tried to kill my friends. And that . . ." I looked at Finch, and he looked at me, and our eyes held. "That. Is. Not. Him."

Chaos.

Shouts and yells and whispers and echoes, *what are they doing here, strangers, they need to leave, Pastor Walker Rose, leave, leave, leave.*

And above it all Duncan Begg telling people to be quiet.

I looked behind me.

Neely wasn't there.

River, where the hell did your brother go?

"Who are you, girl? Where did you come from?" Duncan Begg's eyes were on me now, oh yes they were.

I couldn't see Neely anywhere.

I started walking down the aisle toward Duncan, and my mouth opened and words started spilling out like they'd given up hope on me and were trying to get out while they could. "The real devil-boy is named Brodie. He's from Texas and wears a cowboy hat. He can do things with his mind, make people see things. He has red hair, just the same color red as that boy's, but—"

"Shut your mouth, girl." Drood, the man with the sores, dragged the last word out, long and slow. He pointed at me, and then at Aggie, with his thick finger. "Looks like what we've got here is some redhead-boy sympathizers. You know what my grandmother always told me? She said witches love red hair, red as the setting sun. The redder the better. And she said they can't stand to see a true reddie harmed. She said they'll band together to rescue one in danger. That's how you can catch yourself a bundle of witches—threaten to hang a reddie and they'll come right to your door. So here's what I think. I think we need to have a hanging tonight, and a burning, just like in the old days—"

That's when the yelling started.

Aggie and her husband stood up and started backing toward the doors.

Drood moved toward Aggie, the whole crowd moved toward Aggie.

Maybe Brodie had left, maybe he was long gone, but the whole town was still sparked, he'd sparked them up, they had to be sparked, this wasn't normal, even for a backwoods forgotten town with a Duncan Begg. Brodie ran and left poor Finch in his place to take the blame, that's exactly what he would do, let some other boy get burned, oh, how that would make him laugh—

And that's when I saw him. Neely, slipping through the shadows, hugging the wall, moving toward Finch. I saw the ropes around Finch's wrists fall away, and Finch's hand reach out . . .

. . . and I ran up, and took it, and then Pine was there, and she was pointing to a small side door half hidden in the shadows and then Pine was pulling me through and I was pulling on Finch's hand and Neely followed behind all of us and then we were out in the snow. We ran to the side of the church and Finch bolted up the steps and shoved a thick tree branch through the front door handles just in time and the people inside began to bang and scream, and I heard the wood splinter, but then we were gone, gone, gone.

Luke had the car running. Sunshine was sitting in the front seat and I pushed Finch into the back between Neely and me, and *go, go, go.*

But there was Pine standing stock-still in the beam of the headlights, wearing her little home-sewn dress and black boots and my striped scarf.

Hurry, Vi, hurry, they're coming, damn it, hurry . . .

"You can come with," I said, quick, quick, quick, trying not to look over my shoulder at the woods spreading toward town. "You can come with us. Just—just get in. *Hurry . . .*"

Pine's gray eyes were shiny and big in the winter moonlight. "Not yet," she whispered. "Not yet."

And there wasn't time, and Sunshine was screaming *Vi, Vi, Vi,* and I said, "Will you be okay? Will they hurt you for helping us?"

But Pine just shrugged and shook her head and then Luke screamed, *"Violet, I hear them,"* and so I jumped in the car and said, GO.

Luke threw the car in reverse and we all lurched sideways in our seats. I leaned to the side and rolled down the window—

"Come to Citizen Kane, it's up north, by the sea, in a town called Echo . . ." and Pine nodded quick and fast and then Luke spun the car out of the trees.

I turned and looked out the rear window, and there they came, the people of Inn's End, running out of the woods, sweeping Pine up in their wake, running, running straight toward us.

But we'd already reached Witch William's bridge and they were too damn late.

CHAPTER 9

December

Will walked in on us. Lucas was kneeling at my feet and asking me to marry him.

I was bad. Will was bad. Lucas was good.

Sometimes life is that simple.

Will stood in the doorway and stared at me, and then down at Lucas, and his eyes were full of the flash, the flash that screamed burn, burn, burn.

Lucas, his knees by my feet, his shoulders solid and his eyes steady.

I said yes.

Will raged and raged and raged and raged.

Later that night Lucas fell down the grand

staircase on his way to dinner and broke his arm in three places.

≈≈≈

After we crossed the bridge, after we took turn after turn after turn, we landed on a paved road again. Finch leaned into me and fell asleep, just like that. He smelled like dirt and snow and fear, but I didn't mind. In the front seat Sunshine sat snug with Luke, her brown hair cascading over his right arm as his hand clutched the steering wheel. Neely was on the other side of Finch, looking over his red head at me, and smiling every once in a while like nothing at all had happened.

I was still shaking and far from sleep, so I clicked on a flashlight and read the next entry in Freddie's diary.

But it just stirred me up, rather than calming me down.

We hadn't found River. We hadn't found Brodie.

But we'd saved a kid from being strung up and bled dry by a sparked-up stranger-hating town with dead birds on its doors and blood on its gravestones.

So that was something.

I turned off the flashlight. The car went dark except for the lights from the dashboard and the blue predawn outside. Every time I closed my eyes I began to feel that it hadn't been real, none of it, but then I'd open them again and there he was right next to me, red hair on my shoulder. My Inn's End souvenir.

Dawn broke, and Luke pulled over at the first sizeable town. I liked it on sight—it had so many trees squeezing between its clean streets, it seemed about to burst. We parked by the university and piled out to look for food and coffee and shake off Inn's End as much as we could.

The university was white and shining and beautiful and old and regal and proud, and I thought it was just the kind of college I wanted to go to and maybe I would. Someday I wouldn't be Devil hunting and then I would have time to think about applications and pamphlets and Go Wildcats or Cavaliers or Vikings.

There were coffee carts stationed where the sidewalks ended, still open even with the holidays, run by students that loved to talk joe. Which I'd missed doing since Gianni at the café back home had stopped speaking to me after that night with tied-up Jack and the fire in the Glenship attic. I looked around and imagined professors strolling by looking pleased with themselves and full of things to say, and kids carrying books and backpacks and wearing fat knit scarves. The sun was out and Inn's End already seemed like a damn half dream.

We bought coffee from three of the four carts and then sat down on the stone steps of the library. Everyone looked red-eyed and shaky and pale, but the coffee would help, soon enough. That, and the bright light of day.

"Riddle," I said, quiet, almost under my breath.

Luke and Sunshine sat next to each other, their knees touching. Sunshine's hair looked soft and pretty in the early light. Luke kept running his hand over it, like he thought so too, or like he was trying to keep her calm.

"It's close," Luke said.

"Close to Echo," Sunshine added, her eyes big, and dark.

"Jack," I said. "All I can think about is Jack. If it's Brodie in that barn . . ."

I turned to Neely, but he was already shaking his head. "I'm going to North Carolina. Sea god, haunted shack—I'll get to the bottom of it. Wide-Eyed Theo's devil-boy story proved true, in the end, and . . . and River always had a fascination with the Outer Banks, ever since we spent a summer there as kids, in a house built on stilts right into the sand." He paused. "So. You coming with, Vi, or you going north?"

Neely smiled like he didn't give a damn about my answer, and then tipped his coffee cup back so he could get the last drop.

But I caught the look in his eyes.

And I saw it, plain as day.

His blue eyes were twinkling, but underneath that

twinkle . . . he wanted me to come with. I saw it, damn it all.

"Yes," I answered. Just like that. "I'll go with you."

Neely grinned.

Luke and Sunshine stared at me.

I could feel Finch's gaze on me too. His brown eyes looked different now that there wasn't fear in them. He was still covered in twigs and leaves and looking like he'd been raised by wolves, but his expression was strangely . . . peaceful.

"No," Luke said. "No, Vi. You hunted a devil and found another redheaded orphan to bring back to the Citizen. We're done here. We need to go home, and look into this barn boy, and make sure Jack is safe."

Sunshine tucked her chin into the thick cornflower-blue scarf she was wearing in great folds around her neck, and didn't look me in the eye. "You put all of us in danger at Inn's End, Violet, and what about Jack and your parents, alone at the Citizen? Even if the Riddle story isn't true, Brodie could be anywhere"—her words were going fast, fast, faster—"he could be crawling through your house right now, hiding in closets, and watching, watching, just like last time. We shouldn't have left, we shouldn't have—"

"Hey," Neely said. I saw the fingers on his right hand

twitch. "We all chose to go on this road trip with Violet, Sunshine. She didn't keep anything from us. We all heard Wide-Eyed Theo's story, whether or not we believed it. And I, for one, have no intention of running back to Echo. Not yet. My gut tells me to go to North Carolina. And I have the car. So who's in?"

Neely wants me to come with him, River.

Freddie, and now me—

We can't seem to turn down a Redding, with or without the glow.

"I'm in," I said. Just like that. Again.

"No," Luke said. "No, you're not, Vi."

"I *am,* Luke." I held his damn gaze, didn't flinch, didn't blink. "It's not about choosing North Carolina over Jack. It's about not knowing where the threat is. We have no idea where Brodie and River are. You and Sunshine need to go to Riddle. And you need to stop at Citizen Kane on the way and make sure Jack is all right. But I have to go to this island."

Quiet. A raven flew overhead, and I watched its shadow float over the brick walkway.

My wrists started throbbing again. I rubbed them with my thumbs. Luke and Sunshine wouldn't look me in the eye. Finch sat on his step and was stoic and calm.

Neely stood up finally, and stretched, his back arching

toward the blue sky. "Then it's decided. Luke and Sunshine, you'll follow the barn boy rumor. Take the train back north, get as far as you can, and then call for a ride or hitchhike the rest."

Luke stood up too, and looked at the clock that hung high up on the library wall. "Fine. We don't have time to argue. But if Brodie's really back in Maine and something happens to Jack . . ." He paused, and his eyes met mine. "You'll never forgive yourself, Vi."

I nodded. Because he was right.

I looked up at Neely—his tall body was lean and graceful, framed by trees and white columns.

"But I'm still going with Neely," I said. For the third time.

Luke gave me one last, long look, and then pulled Sunshine to her feet. They started walking back to the car.

Neely went to get another coffee.

Finch stayed where he was, staring off at nothing.

"And what will you do?" I asked, sitting down beside him, so close his red hair touched my shoulder. "You can't go back to Inn's End. You could stay here in this town, I guess, if you wanted. It seems nice. But you can come with us too. We're going to look for a sea god and a haunted hut in North Carolina. Long story."

I paused.

"Or you can go back to the Citizen, with my brother. It's a crumbling mansion on the sea with seven or eight guest bedrooms and you can stay as long as you like. You can help Luke keep an eye on our cousin Jack. I worry about him."

Finch turned his head and looked right at me, and his eyes were deep and feral and . . . *wild* . . . suddenly.

Those wild eyes reminded me a bit of someone.

River.

Cooking me supper last summer, the heat from the pan making his hair stick to his forehead, and he'd looked over his shoulder at me, and smiled, and there was something fierce there, something hungry and held back and . . .

Finch crossed his arms and leaned into the step behind him, and tilted his face to the sun. "I've never seen the sea. I'd like go with you and . . . ?"

"Neely."

"With you and Neely, to North Carolina," he said, his words soft. "And so I guess I will, if that's all right with you."

And that was that.

≈≈≈

There was a 10:00 A.M. train going north. The rosy-cheeked woman at the train station counter was cheerful and energetic—she offered us free coffee from a silver urn on a table near the door, and it was dark and hot and good.

I unfolded a hundred-dollar-bill origami mouse and gave it to her in exchange for two train tickets.

I had three River-animals left in my pocket. I'd never considered myself sentimental, but I really hated parting with the little folded creatures. They meant something. More than money.

I held out the tickets to Luke, plus the leftover cash the ticket woman had given me. He took both, and said nothing.

Finch was quiet in the station lobby, just eyes eyes eyes, taking in the hustle and bustle like it was the circus come to town instead of just regular people moving around in a neat red building with a dozen wooden benches and white columns out front.

But then, I'd never been in a train station either. I kept picturing the movie *Brief Encounter* and wished I could order a cup of tea with sugar in the spoon.

People were beginning to stare at Finch, at his leaves and twigs and dirt.

"Here." Neely handed some of his rich-boy things to Finch and the redheaded ex–Inn's Ender went off and changed in the train station bathroom. He came out with his face washed and his hair brushed sleek and shining. He fit into the clothes well, his shoulders wide and his spine straight, even if the pants were a bit long. He looked like some trust fund kid on his way to a private prep school . . . except for the feeling of wilderness about him, of wide-open skies and long twilights and quiet and dirt-under-the-fingernails and waking-up-all-alone-every-day.

Finch seemed older suddenly, all cleaned up. I thought he might be seventeen, not the fifteen I'd first thought. I'd have to ask him, once I knew him better.

We moved out onto the wooden platform, and then, in a blink, the black train was pulling up and good-byes, good-byes.

"Last chance, Violet," Luke said. He stood on the bottom step of the train and looked down at me. Sunshine was already inside, having walked right by without a word.

I shook my head.

Luke sighed. "Be careful, sister." And his face told me how much he meant it. "I was . . . a coward, back at Inn's End. I'm not proud of it, Vi. But you're making the wrong choice. You are. If a person goes looking for trouble, they'll find it." The train began to howl. "What if the barn boy is River?" he shouted over the noise. "What if it's Brodie? What will we do then?"

I didn't answer.

What would any of us do with either Redding boy if we found him? I hadn't figured that out yet. Sometimes it just wasn't worth thinking ahead. Because then you'd freeze and never end up doing anything, anything at all.

Luke stared at me, and I stared at him, and I could see he was pissed, and sad, and a little scared still. But mainly, mainly he just seemed kind of . . . lost, all of sudden.

"We've never been apart, you know," I said, because we hadn't. But Luke didn't hear me over the howling. He turned and went up the steps.

The train left, and he was gone.

That's when the bad feeling started. Deep in the pit of my belly. Thick and bitter and sweaty.

Luke was right. I'd made the wrong choice.

And I supposed I should have wondered right then if I would ever even see my brother again. But that seemed too dark a thought, even for me.

≈≈≈

We left the college town behind a half hour later, though I didn't want to. The way Inn's End had played out didn't make me all that eager to follow another one of Wide-Eyed Theo's stories down the rabbit hole.

No, that wasn't true. I wanted to go to North Carolina. I did. . . . I just needed one more cup of coffee first.

Finch was quiet as we wandered back through the campus. He didn't seem to understand money very well, let alone have any of his own, so I paid for his coffee and he didn't mind a bit. He winced each time a car went by, and I watched him stand by an overflowing garbage can for a full minute, a melancholy look on his face.

But he watched other people closely and learned fast. The day before, he'd been a cabin-dwelling mountain boy. By the time he'd finished his whole-milk latte, he was leading the way back to the car, cutting through alleys and jaywalking across busy intersections like some true-blue city kid.

"Finch, have you ever been to this town before?" I asked, looking at him out of the corner of my eyes. "Have you ever been anywhere?"

"No." He paused, and glanced around, serious and big-eyed like a deer that had taken a wrong turn and ended up in the middle of town. "The world is a lot bigger than I thought." A truck rambled down the road in front of us. "And a lot louder."

"A lot bigger?" Neely repeated, and laughed. Though not in an unfriendly way. "We haven't even left the state yet. You wait."

And Finch nodded, though I detected a bit of doubt in his eyes, like he wanted to believe Neely about the world being bigger but couldn't yet, not quite.

We got in the car and drove away.

The truth was, I'd been back in civilization and I liked it. The grand university had sucked the Devil-hunting itch right out of me.

I thought about me going east and Luke going north and I felt a tug. Something was going taut between us, some connection, like the one between me and the sea.

"I'd like to hear your story," Finch said from the backseat after we turned down a two-lane road that lazily wound around an orchard-covered hill. A few frozen apples still swung from the bare branches and I was tempted to reach out the window and try to grab one. "I haven't talked to other people in a long time and I like listening to your voice."

I took off my seat belt and turned to face him. "I was just about to ask you to do the same thing."

"You first," he said back, half smiling at me in that strange, contrasting way he had, gentle and wild all at once, like a caged wolf only half resigned to his fate. I guess that's what came from growing up all alone in the forest. He had a dimple on his left cheek, a deep one. I decided right then that dimples were inherently likeable.

I told Finch about me, and Luke, and Sunshine, and Neely and Freddie and Citizen Kane and what happened last summer and how we ended up in Inn's End. I wasn't used to talking so much at once, and it didn't come easily to me, but I got better as I went along. Finch was quiet, his expression mild, and I would have thought he didn't believe me at all, believe my tale of glow and spark and blood and fire, except his eyes never left mine.

We went by bare, brown vineyards, their grapes stolen for wine. We went by farms, red barns and dark fences and endless trees. I told Finch about River. And about Brodie. I talked about the red hair and the knife and the cowboy and the mad mother and him cutting up Jack and him biting River and how it ended when I stabbed him in the chest as I bled to death out my wrists.

I showed him the scars and he touched each with his right finger, softly. "I'm sorry about this," he said, leaving his finger on my left wrist and looking me straight in the eye. "I wish I had been there. I wish I could have saved you the way you saved me in Inn's End."

I shook my head. "You couldn't have stopped Brodie."

"And yet you're hunting him." Finch's expression still had that caged look. "What do you plan to do if you find him?"

I could feel Neely look at me. I moved my wrist away from Finch's hand. "If we find Brodie, then . . . then I'll . . . I'll stab him again. With a knife this time, not a shard of glass. And this time I'll kill him."

Finch's eyebrows went up. Just slightly. But I saw it. He doubted me.

Of course he doubted me.

River, what am I going to do if we find Brodie in North Carolina instead of you?

"I'd like to see this Citizen Kane someday," Finch said

after I was quiet for a while. "I'd like to have coffee in the guesthouse and dig up old clothes in the attic."

"You can," I said, trying not to sound too excited. I can't help getting excited when anyone seems interested in the Citizen. "Once we finish up in North Carolina, you can come back with Neely and me and see it all for yourself and stay as long as you like."

Finch nodded, and his mouth broke into a sweet, genuine smile. He reached forward and grabbed my hands, putting his fingertips on my wrists again. "So which one are we going to find in North Carolina?" he asked, after a moment. "River, or Brodie?"

"I don't know." Outside, the landscape had flattened, and lost some of its trees. "Probably neither."

Neely looked at me again, quick, and then turned back to the road. "River loves the Outer Banks," he called behind him to Finch. "It was the first place he ran away to back when he was fifteen."

"But a sea god sounds more like Brodie." I paused, and slipped my hands out of Finch's grasp. "Either way, if a Redding boy is there, we'll find him."

"You can only run so far on an island." Finch sat back in his seat and put his arms behind his head.

"Do you mean us, or them?" I asked.

But Finch just shrugged. His eyes held mine, and . . .

shifted. They lit up, and I saw curiosity shining inside them, sparkly and bright, like stars in a moonless sky.

"I'm looking forward to the sea," he said, and smiled again.

≈≈≈

We reached the coast just as the sun started going down. I drank in the sight of the sea, breathed in the smell of it. I rolled down the window so the breeze could tangle up my hair.

Neely parked the car on a side street in the small coastal town of Nags Dune. We got out and walked right down to the water. Neely stood by me with his legs apart, hands on hips, and looked very Mr. Adventure. But it was Finch I was watching. If he'd never seen the ocean, then I wanted to see how he took it. I couldn't imagine being fifteen or possibly seventeen and never having been to the Great Big Blue. It was such a part of me, like my name and the color of my hair.

Finch faced the sea with his back straight and his palms turned out. He batted his eyes and breathed deep and I kind of felt like hugging him.

"How old are you, Finch?" I asked.

"Seventeen," he answered. "I think. Not really sure." And then he turned his face back to the water and disappeared into the experience of it again.

I thought about what Aggie had said, about him losing his mother and then his grandmother too. I wondered how long he'd been alone.

And then I wondered if Aggie had survived the night.

And Pine . . . after we left her there, standing in the middle of the road . . . Did they let her keep my scarf, or did they take it away?

Did they figure out that she helped us?

Don't think about it, Vi. Don't. There was nothing you could do.

But my heart was racing and I felt kind of sick. I forced myself to take big sea breaths, over and over.

The ferries had stopped running for the day and the sun was sinking fast. I thought we'd have to camp on the beach. I even set my heart on it. I wanted to crawl into Neely's tent and stop caring about everything and have the waves sing us to sleep like the wolves in the wilderness of New York.

But then a man with rugged red cheeks and kind blue eyes and thick working-man's fingers wandered up to us after a few minutes and asked where we were going.

"We're trying to find a fisherman's shack," Neely said, lifting his hand to his forehead to shield his eyes from the last sharp rays of the sun.

The man laughed, and his eyes crinkled at the sides. "Well, the coast is full of those," he said.

"This one's haunted."

He just looked at us, a smile flickering at the corners of his mouth.

"How about an island with wild horses?" I asked.

The seafarer nodded, like he was in familiar territory now. "Carollie, then?"

Was there more than one island with wild horses?

"Sure," Neely answered, because we didn't know any better anyway.

Our new sea captain introduced himself as Hayden. He gave us a long look as he shook our hands, and told us it would be ten dollars a head.

Which was fair and all right, but I was running out of River's money, damn it. Fast. I unfolded another origami creature and handed it over.

Hayden had a small boat, just big enough for him and us. We left the car behind in Nags Dune, parked in a lot behind a hardware store. We took our suitcases and camping gear and the picnic basket and strode down a dock to a boat that looked as strong and weather-beaten as its owner.

The open sea.

For a girl who's lived her whole life footsteps from the ocean, you'd think I would have set foot on a big sea-crossing boat at some point. But the Whites barely had enough money to pay the taxes on Citizen Kane, and buy canvases and paints. There was nothing left over for yacht buying. Freddie had talked about going to boat parties when she was young, and I'd listened closely and pretty much felt like I'd spent my youth yachting on the sea too. But the actual truth was that I was a girl born by the ocean who'd never ever done the *Queen Mary,* or anything even close.

The three of us stood in the red boat, all together in a line, the dark twilight water moving under our feet and splashing us in the face. Hayden's hair was cropped close and his eyes were permanently narrowed from staring into the sun all day. He held the wheel and looked over at us occasionally in a puzzled sort of way.

"I was born on a yacht," Neely said, after the houses and shops on the shore had become nothing but twinkling lights in the distance.

I knew Neely was an old hand at this traveling-by-sea thing, but this was news. "No you weren't," I said, and smiled.

"River's the liar, remember?" He smiled back. "I came early. My parents were sailing to the Azores and my mother went into labor. My father delivered me with the help of the ship's cook. My mother said later that River kept crying and calling out for her, but he stopped the second he saw me for the first time. I always . . ."

Neely didn't finish his sentence. His voice faded into the sound of the waves splitting to let Hayden's boat through. He moved toward me, just an inch or two, just until our arms touched.

Finch turned and looked at Neely. "When did she die?"

Neely raised his eyebrows at him in a "how did you know?" way.

"I heard it in your voice," Finch said. He leaned his lower back against the side of the boat.

Neely wiped a few drops of seawater off his forehead and stared at the dark horizon. "A while ago. Five years."

Finch nodded. "And your father?"

"Still alive," was all Neely said.

Silence.

"You kids know what you're doing, going to Carollie this time of year?" Hayden asked a few minutes later. He was still throwing glances our way, and looking a little worried. I wondered if he had children at home. I pictured him with a strong sea wife, curly hair flying in the wind, her face pretty and clear except for the wrinkles settling in near her eyes from too much staring out at the ocean and thinking about her husband being at its mercy.

"No," Neely called out, with a laugh, back to his old self.

"But we're going anyway. Why? What's the matter with Carollie this time of year?"

But Hayden had turned his gaze back to the water and didn't answer.

And the next thing we knew he was pulling up to another dock and the long sandy beach of Carollie stretched out in front of us, blue-black under the blue-black sky.

And, just as our feet hit the sand, we saw them. Dark shapes running through the dusk ahead of us, kicking up their heels, heads high in the air.

Wild horses.

"They're descended from horses that survived a shipwreck," Hayden said. "They swam to this island and have lived here ever since."

We all watched the horses run for a while, their bodies flying through the dark, tails swishing, not giving a damn about anything else in the whole world.

I felt something release inside of me then. Something I hadn't known I'd been holding on to. It ripped through my body and I shuddered as it left.

CHAPTER 10

HAYDEN TOLD US that the only place to get supper was "at the Hag's Shack down the shore, near the town." Everything else was closed for the season.

We could see the Hag's Shack lights from where we stood. The small town glimmered behind it, like a smattering of stars dripping down the beach. The three of us said good-bye to Hayden, and then headed toward the glow, the wild horses still beating a path down the beach behind us.

Finch carried the sleeping bags and tents and he seemed overburdened, despite his strong arms and straight back. But when I asked him if he was all right, he gave me a quick glance and a quicker smile and said he enjoyed the labor of it.

Neely walked next to me, whistling like he hadn't a care in the world, because nothing really kept Neely down, did it.

And I was in a good mood too. I was by the ocean again. And the ocean meant home. The waves didn't crash here like they did on Citizen Kane's bit of rocky shore, but it felt reassuring, nevertheless.

The Hag's Shack was a small little seafood place off by itself on the sand. It looked like it had been built from a large shipping crate, metal and blue and rectangular. It had an open-air counter where you ordered your food and then ate it standing up or sitting on the deck, your feet dangling off the edge. Without the sun, the air was cold, but there was a fire burning in a black fire pit, and that kept things warm enough.

The menu was handwritten on a chalkboard, big and clear. There were a few locals in front of us, and I watched them for signs of Inn's End–ishness. But they just looked like hungry people anywhere, tired at the end of a long day and anxious to put food in their bellies. If they noticed that we strangers were cuddling up to their seafood shack, they didn't seem to care.

The girl behind the counter was the only employee about the place. She was curvy like Sunshine, but shorter, and had dark, curly black hair, a round face, childlike rosebud lips, and feisty eyes. She took our order for three Vietnamese coffees and three clam chowders and three fried oyster tacos and a seared tuna salad, all while jumping between the register and the sizzling pieces of fish she was flipping on the grill.

We ate by the outdoor fire, lemony sauce dripping through our fingers. And it was all hot and good, good, good, the fish tender and salty, the coffee smooth and sweet.

Two local boys joined us after a few minutes—both with thick, dark brown hair and big smiles and a cocky, graceful way of holding their shoulders back and tilting their chins up. Brothers, no doubt. They were as pretty as a pair of Greek gods and they knew it too. They made eyes at every female between them and the counter, and they even winked at me. I noticed they didn't flirt with the fish-frying girl, though. They put in their order and then leaned forward and whispered to her in a serious, intimate way—no smiles, no winks.

When we finished eating we just stayed where we were by the fire. We had nowhere else to go. The place slowly cleared out. Two shiny-cheeked girls joined the Greek god boys and eventually they all swaggered off, laughing.

I wondered if Neely would let me sleep in his tent again.

I wondered if the horses would trample us as we dreamed.

I wouldn't mind that, not as much as you'd think.

"You need a place to stay?" The curly-haired girl had broken free from her counter and stood looking at us where we sat by the fire, eyeing up our suitcases and camping gear.

"What makes you think that?" Neely asked, and laughed his chuckling, contagious laugh. He stood up and reached out his hand. "I'm Neely. The blonde there is Vi and the redhead is Finch. We thought we'd camp here on the beach. Hotels are out—we blew through our money on coffee, gas, and train tickets. Long story."

The girl nodded. "I'm Canto," she said, shaking our hands. She had taken her apron off and wore a red sweater and black knee-high socks and a skirt with a dolphin stitched on it. "You can stay at my place for a while, if you want. It's free, provided you help a bit with cleaning and cooking. If you're lazy and you don't want to work, then don't bother. I hate lazy people and can't stand to be around them. But otherwise, what's mine is yours."

Finch, who had been silent until now, standing back in the shadows, stepped forward. "Yes," he said, calm and bold as you please. "We aren't lazy and we'll take it."

"Agreed," Neely added.

That was quick, I thought.

Canto was pretty and round and sure of herself and full

of opinions on lazy people. And we didn't have anywhere else to go.

Still . . . it annoyed me a little, how fast the boys said yes. It did.

"Well, I'm kind of lazy," I said.

But Canto just smiled and shook her head, thick curls flopping about her ears and shoulders. She leaned in and stared at me with sharp black eyes. "You don't look lazy," she said. And it seemed to be enough for her.

We helped her close up the Hag's Shack. Neely washed dishes and I scrubbed the grill and Finch packed the left-over fish on fresh ice. We left the fire to burn out on its own and then followed Canto into the town, which had the same name as the island, Carollie. It was small, just a smattering of houses and a couple of crisscrossing streets. Smaller than my hometown, Echo, but bigger than Inn's End. Most of the shops and restaurants on the main street were closed, as Hayden had said, it being the off-season. Still, we walked by what looked like an active café. One that opened the next morning at six. Perfect.

"Really?" I said. And then again. "Really?" Because we'd gotten to Canto's house. It was at the end of town, on stilts like the Hag's Shack, and facing the ocean. And it was . . . huge. Not as big as Citizen Kane, with its seven or eight guest bed-rooms and two main staircases, but still. Huge.

The house was weathered and ramshackle. The wood was a tough, sea-beaten gray, and it had a boxy four-story tower and bay windows and multiple decks and stairs descending into the sand. Several tiny blue shutters covered several small windows and it was pointed and gabled and a hundred years old if it was a day. It looked full of forgotten corners and nooks and crannies and ghosts and moaning sea captain widows. The ocean was lapping at its feet, and *damn,* if there was ever a house that belonged to the sea as much as Citizen Kane, this was it.

We walked up some rickety steps and across a rickety deck and then we squeezed through a door and stumbled into a large room. Canto flipped on the lights, with a snappy little *ta-da,* and I set down my suitcase and looked around.

Comfortable couches and wicker chairs and sunflower curtains and mismatched everything. There was dust on the fireplace mantel and cobwebs swinging from the ceiling and books piled up on the floor. It was cold, no fire in the fireplace, no heat running through the radiators. Sand crunched underneath my feet where it hadn't been swept up in a while.

And the walls were painted pale green. Freddie's color. Like this was right. Like it was meant to be.

"You live here all alone, don't you," I said, because

suddenly I just knew. I felt it, like I felt the sea swirling about right outside. I was so familiar with living parentless in a big house that I would have known blindfolded.

Canto tilted her head and gave me an odd look. "Yes. I do. My mother died when I was little and my dad is out at sea nine months of the year." She paused, and seemed to read something in my face that made her keep talking. "Sometimes he forgets to send money and that's why I work at the Hag's Shack seven days a week."

And she shrugged, like it was nothing.

But in that shrug I saw bills unpaid. Holidays spent alone. No letters or postcards. And the wondering, always the wondering.

I didn't say anything, and she didn't say anything, and we both knew anyway. We could smell it on each other like some hopeful, melancholy cologne.

Two peas in a pod. Us.

But then Canto grinned, and there was a different feeling about her suddenly. A lighter feeling. She spread her arms wide and threw her head back.

"Welcome to Captain Nemo. Sometimes I take in travelers and make them pay rent, but I won't charge you guys as long as you help out. I've gotten really behind, trying to run the Shack and go to school at the same time." Canto tapped her foot against the warped hardwood floor and it crunched. "Someone needs to sweep tomorrow. I vote Finch. He looks strong enough to empty this house of sand."

Finch looked at her, a sweet, woodland expression on his face. "I'll see what I can do," he said. And suddenly the sweet expression faded and his eyes went wild and I saw his dimple pop out, so he wasn't hiding as much as he thought he was.

Canto nodded at Finch, and then smiled. Maybe she saw the dimple too. "Good. Don't disappoint me. My dad says my tongue is sharper than a shark's hunger and he knows what he's talking about. He almost lost his leg off the coast of Australia, caught between a tiger shark's teeth."

That smacks of bullshit, I thought. And then realized I didn't really care.

Canto walked through the living room and started down a short hallway, flipping on more lights. "Go ahead and explore. Pick a bedroom. Mine is on the top floor of the tower, but everything else is fair game. I'll get a fire going in the fireplace and then we can have some hot caramel milk. And while we drink it we can tell each other our stories."

"Can you put some coffee in that caramel?" Neely called down, already ten steps up what I figured must be the way to the tower.

"You drink too much coffee," Canto yelled from the kitchen at the end of the hall, though how she knew this I didn't know. "You'll drink my caramel milk straight and you'll like it."

And Neely laughed and laughed, all the way up the stairs.

CHAPTER 11

February

William was coming apart at the seams. Burning up from the inside.

His family was richer than God now. They owned everything. Factories. Ships. Islands. All that burning. I told him there would be a price. There's always a price.

Chase Glenship swaggered back home from a couple of months abroad. We left the city to come and meet him. He was filled to bursting with stories and worldly wisdom so fresh and new it was practically still in the box.

That night, after everyone was asleep, even the servants, he dragged us all up to the attic and showed us the pipes and things he'd bought off a sailor in Greece. He was a true Byron.

I loved the Glenship attic, the angles and cobwebs. I wanted to have an attic just like it someday. Someday I would leave New York City and move to Echo for good. Lucas had promised, earnest, solemn, to build me a house on the sea, like the Glenship, and let me have it exactly the way I wanted. He was already building it, in fact. And was paying the workers double to hurry, in case I changed my mind.

Will's sister, Rose, sat on a sofa in the corner. She was flushed and excited, and Lucas sat next to her, stoic and tolerant, as usual.

I had on my new yellow dress. It was slinky and daring and heavy with beaded fringe. Will said it made my gams look too skinny. He would say that.

Chase stood in the center of the attic floor in his white suit and dared me to do it. To smoke the Oriental poppy. So I did.

Afterward we went for a swim in the Glenship's underground pool, naked as the day we were born. When I started stripping down to my skivvies, Lucas took Rose and left.

The world was a sweet, dreamy blue mist. I slipped out of the water and put on a pair of Chase's trousers and belted them tight to my waist. I buttoned one of his starched shirts too, right over my breasts, nothing underneath. I started walking into town. The boys followed.

We ended up at the church. The doors were locked even though church doors were always open back then. But Chase had a key. Of course he had a key.

It was a small, white building with Hawthorne gables. We went in. I stretched out across a wooden pew, and wiggled my toes. I was barefoot. Where were my shoes? Had I walked into town without shoes? Or had I left them underneath a pew somewhere?

Then Will was kissing me, kissing my neck, warming me up, right there with God watching. Burn and opium. Opium and burn. Maybe Chase kissed me too. Maybe they were both kissing me when the priest found us.

He leaned over me and said I was a drugged Jezebel blaspheming God in his home. He said I was Eve with the apple, and the snake too.

He said nothing to the boys. Even Chase, who

he knew from the occasional repentant Sunday. I think that's what angered Will the most. He pushed the priest away from me. Hard.

That night, long after we'd crawled into our beds to dream the dreams of the hell-bent young, the priest set the church on fire, with himself inside.

And that's when I knew how bad it was.

≈≈≈

The bedroom I picked on the second tower floor of Captain Nemo had a treasure map theme. A large compass had been painted on one of the yellow walls, pointing north, followed by a trail of black slashes that went all around the big room and its big bay window, leading to a big black *X*. I wondered if Canto was behind the theme, and thinking so made me like her even more.

The bed was soft and there was sand in the corners and dust on the warped wood dresser and the bay window had a comfy window seat where someone could sit and read and look out to sea. So I sat down right there, read the next entry in Freddie's diary, and then closed the book, slam.

Citizen Kane's library had a rare, seven-volume horror collection—I read the series straight through one lonely winter. In one story, the main character found a diary left by a dead cousin. It gave clues and spilled secrets and solved mysteries. But. But it also stirred up trouble and opened old wounds and made the main character think she didn't really ever know a person, not a bit, not at all.

Part of me wished I would have remembered this story, about the diary, before I started reading Freddie's.

I thought about the burn, and the glow, and Will Redding going mad with it, and River going mad with it, and Freddie wrapped up in it, just like I was.

I got up and went to see what rooms the boys chose. Neely took the other bedroom on the second floor—it had striped wallpaper coming loose in spots, and two black trunks filled with old sea maps and charts.

Finch was in a bird-themed room on the top floor. Bird knickknacks and bird wallpaper and feeders were hanging outside the windows.

I peeked into Canto's room while I was up there, since the door was open. It was cluttered with clothes and books and a sewing machine. Half-finished skirts and dresses were thrown over worn chairs near the windows. Bowls filled with pretty beachcombing finds like seashells and polished glass sat on every free windowsill and dresser. I felt someone behind me, and turned around. Finch was standing there, taking a peek into Canto's room too. He must have liked what he saw, since his damn dimple showed itself again.

We gathered in the living room by the fire, Canto and Finch and me on the floor, Neely in a ragged, rusty-orange loveseat, one elbow crooked around one knee, leaning back. His skin looked smooth and soft like someone who got way more sleep than he did, and drank way less coffee.

I poured myself a cup of caramel milk. My mug was thick, white on the inside, brown on the outside, and missing its handle. The drink was earthy and sweet. I tasted salt on the back of my tongue. I wasn't sure if Canto had added salt to the caramel or if it was just in the air. Everything on this island was salty, much more so than Echo—after all, the ocean sloshed against the stilts underneath the floorboards I sat on. If a person swiped his finger down the mantel and licked it, I'd bet the deed on Citizen Kane that the dust would taste like sea salt.

"So why are you here?" Canto asked, blunt, no hesitation. "No one comes to Carollie in the winter."

"We're here to find the sea god," I said, betraying my hard-earned Agatha Christie wisdom. But Canto seemed like the kind of girl who wanted the truth straight up and in her face anyway. "We heard a rumor that a North Carolina island was worshiping a sea god, and we came to see what was what. He . . . we think this sea god could be a friend of ours."

Neely leaned in closer to watch her face, and then, a second later, Finch did the same.

Canto's dark eyebrows bunched up, and she smiled a puzzled half smile, like she thought we were joking. "A *sea god*? Who told you this?"

"A late-night radio program called *Stranger Than Fiction*," Neely answered with a confident, cocky grin, like he'd just said "*The New York Times.*"

Canto took a sip of the caramel, swallowed. "*Stranger Than Fiction*? That sounds reliable. What time is this show on? Wait, let me guess . . . three in the morning?"

Neely laughed. "Don't knock it till you've tried it."

Finch made a small sound, kind of a *hmmm.* He was sitting to Canto's right, watching everything she did from the corners of his eyes.

"Speak up, Finch," Canto said, tilting her face to look at him.

"He said," I interrupted, when Finch didn't answer, "that the radio show has been right before."

Finch nodded, once, slowly, the tips of his red hair brushing his chin.

"There was another North Carolina story too," I added, when Finch still didn't talk. "A haunted fisherman's hut. Teenagers go in and never come out again."

Canto's eyes snapped on mine. "That story is bullshit."

I perked up. "What story?"

"Oh, that the Lillian Hut is haunted. A long time ago a fisherman named Clayton Lillian strangled his sister Winks Lillian with a piece of fishing line in a shack by the sea. And then he disappeared. People won't go near it now. But the hut is right down this beach a ways and I've walked by it a thousand times and nothing has ever happened to me. It's just an abandoned shack."

I met Neely's gaze.

I knew where we were going tomorrow.

I opened my mouth to ask a few follow-up questions, but before I could frame a sentence, Canto pushed her thick curls back from her face, stuck a short finger out, and pointed to Finch. "You. Tell me your story. I don't think you belong to these other two." She turned to point at Neely and me. "At least, you haven't for long."

Neely laughed and started rubbing his right forearm with his left hand in an absent way. "You'll want to keep an eye on this one," he said, speaking to me but looking at Canto. "She's doesn't miss a thing."

"Yeah, I noticed." There was a bit of gloom in my voice. And I guess if I thought about it long enough, I might have figured where it came from and why it was there.

So I didn't think about it.

"I have no story," Finch said. His voice was low, with a

throaty, hoarse quality that reminded me of scratchy old records playing in the Citizen's attic. "When I was eight years old my mother went deep into the forest to gather wintergreen berries and I never saw her again. Who knows who my father was. I was raised by my grandmother Owl Grieve. Sometimes I went to Inn's End for school, but mostly not. My grandmother died and then it was just me. Chopping wood and walking through snow and making rabbit stew. And the sun rising and setting and the seasons passing. And that's it." He paused. "There's nothing else to say."

I was impressed. Canto ordered Finch to open up, and he did.

"You must have been lonely," I said, mostly to myself.

In twenty-four hours I'd met a boy raised by his grandmother and a girl left alone in a big house. Maybe my life hadn't been as uniquely sad as I'd previously thought.

I guess this is the benefit of travel.

Finch didn't answer me. He was still looking at Canto. "One night I was watching the stars and thinking everything would always be as it always was. Then I was tied up and dragged into the church to be hanged or burned or bled. I was rescued in the nick of time and then taken to the sea. Who knows what will happen next, with the way things are going."

There was a long silence. I leaned back into the sofa behind me and my shoulder brushed by Neely's knee. He didn't move for a second . . . and then I felt his fingers reach through my long hair and stroke my neck. Just the once.

I looked at Canto. "The radio show said Inn's End had a devil-boy stealing girls' dreams. But the real boy had left by the time we got there. The town had decided Finch would be a good enough substitute. They were going to kill him."

"Oh," was all Canto said. No questions about the devil-boy or about a town that executed its own vengeance. But her expression wasn't quite as nonchalant as her mouth. Her black eyes looked thoughtful and her eyebrows bunched up again. She had inched closer and closer to Finch while he talked, until the two of them were sharing the same blanket by the fire, her shoulder touching his.

There was something about Finch. There was something strong and welcoming and . . . *expectant* about him, like a cool autumn breeze blowing across your neck on a hot September day. I was already growing attached to the caged, wild look that slid into his eyes whenever he thought no one was looking—it was charming and cryptic and exactly what I'd expect to find in the eyes of a boy who grew up alone in a forest.

"So what do you think of the world outside Inn's End, Finch?" Neely asked, when he noticed me staring at my Inn's End souvenir. "Does it suit you?"

"It does," Finch answered. "It's less quiet. And a lot more interesting. I think this place is going to be good for me." And he was looking at Canto when he said it.

Canto yawned. She put her hand to her mouth, and the yawn turned into a smile.

"I get up early," she said. "Have to get the fish when it comes in. I'm going to hit the hay. We'll talk more tomorrow night." Here she looked at Neely. "I want to hear more about this friend who may or may not be a sea god."

She waved a good-night to us, walked to the tower stairs, turned, and came back. She slid her fingers into Finch's red hair, and messed it up. "Devil-boy. Right. I think you're all a bunch of liars, and you're the worst of the bunch. Still, thanks for telling us your story."

Finch watched her climb the stairs. I couldn't see his face, but I figured his dimple had popped out again.

The three of us went to bed too, not long after.

I drifted off to sleep in my little treasure map room, listening to the waves lap and feeling a bit of my homesickness drain away. I thought about my brother, and Sunshine. I wondered where they were, if they had made it home yet, if they were scared, if they were hating me for not going with, if it had been the right thing to do, in the end. I was worried about Jack. And I missed Luke. It had only been a day, but knowing he wasn't nearby, that I couldn't walk down the hall or out to the shed and talk to him anytime I wanted . . . it disturbed me in some deep way.

And then my thoughts went to Inn's End as I started sinking into sleep. Inn's End and Finch. I seemed drawn to on-their-own types. Jack, and Finch, and now maybe Canto too. Them and me. Metal and magnet. I guess it was my lot in life, like red-haired, green-gabled Anne, with the twins . . .

≈≈≈

"Violet."

I opened my eyes and turned over. "Hey, Neely," I said at the dark shape standing by the bed. "Is it time for *Stranger Than Fiction*?"

He nodded, and his blond hair flopped around, silver-blue in the moonlight. "But you need to see this first. Hurry," he added, grabbing my hand after I crawled out of bed.

He dragged me over to the bay window.

I blinked several times, and leaned my face against the glass to see better. Neely kept hold of my hand and I let him.

I saw it. A light on the beach. Coming toward the house. Closer. And closer. Right up on the deck. I heard a door open downstairs . . .

Neely's hand was on my mouth before I could say anything. He waited a second, took his hand away, and brought his finger to his lips. I nodded.

The tower stairs creaked. A door opened somewhere above me, and closed again.

Canto.

"She could have been doing anything," I whispered. "Checking fish traps or other fisherwoman things."

"That's true." Neely looked at me, and then grinned. "But, all things considered, what are the odds?"

Despite myself, I grinned back. "The odds are terrible," I whispered.

I sat down on my bed and tucked my knees under my chin and my cold feet underneath my long nightgown. "She wasn't lying, though, when she said she didn't know about the sea god." I let my hair fall over my cold cheeks. "I know she wasn't."

Neely sat down next to me and started rubbing my cold right foot between his warm hands. "Tomorrow we'll find this Lillian Hut. And tomorrow night, if she sneaks out again, we follow Canto. All right?"

I nodded.

Neely warmed up my other foot, and then stood up again. He went over to a beat-up plastic radio on the dresser. Turned it on. Spun dials.

. . . *Eyed Theo. I'm here. You're here. And it's the witching hour. Time for your daily dose of* Stranger Than Fiction.

My only update tonight comes out of the Colorado Rockies. My source, who lives by himself in a cabin and seems to be the rugged mountain-man type, claims the nearby town is acting strange. He said, quote, "All those folks in Gold Hollow have gone stark mad. They keep talking about the trees, saying the trees told them to do this or that, and none of it any good. And now I've heard the children have all gone missing too. They followed a tall, thin, red-haired girl into the mountains and no one's seen them since."

This is a new one, listeners. Talking trees full of bad intentions and a pied piper girl. My source refused to mention any specifics—he said he didn't want to be laughed at on the radio—but he wanted me to send someone out there to investigate, since, quote, "the nearest law is in Boulder and they don't believe me, and won't drive up here anyway because of the snow."

Anyone near Colorado want to do some investigating? I'd owe you one.

It's Wide-Eyed Theo, signing off for the night.

Go forth and find the strange.

"Maybe we should have gone to the mountains, instead of the sea," Neely said, and laughed. "Damn it. I hate being wrong."

"Don't you have a half sister, Neely?"

"Do I?" he asked, quiet.

"You sound like River," I answered, quiet too.

Neely raised one eyebrow and looked so cocky and mischievous and River-like suddenly that my heart started to ache. And then he grinned and it went away.

I met his eyes. "Back in the guesthouse. The day I met you. You said you had two half brothers and one half sister, that you knew about. And the half sister was in Colorado. It could be her, Neely, leading those kids into the woods."

Neely shrugged. "Or it's Brodie in a dress. Or it's just nothing at all." He shrugged and turned the radio off . . .

. . . and the next thing I knew he was pulling his shirt over his head and slipping out of his wool trousers and climbing into my bed and I was climbing in right next to him and picturing those wild horses in my mind and nothing happened except me squeezing myself into his smooth side and resting my head on his shoulder and feeling his soft scar underneath my cheek and my feet nestling in between his warm legs.

Neely whispered, *No wonder River liked this so much,* and heaved a deep sigh, and then both of us, sleep, sleep, sleep.

≈

My dreams were loud. And dark. At first it was just flashes of Neely smiling and the spindly Captain Nemo and Canto with an odd, blank look and Finch swimming in a black sea, his red hair looking redder than the setting sun . . .

But then my dreams turned to River.

River with a glint in his eyes and a gold crown on his head.

River with his arms wide, wild horses behind him, hooves pounding, kicking sand into the air. The sea and the wind and a ragged shack and then he grabbed me and his palms were covered with sand, and I didn't care, it belonged there, and the grains scraped down my skin as he pulled me in, and I was soft and pliable as seaweed in the surf and when River opened his mouth the sounds of the sea came out, crashing and lapping, and the wet, and the blue, and the deep . . .

When I woke in the pre-dawn dark, Neely was still beside me. He was breathing in and out, slow, soft. I let my forehead rest against his warm, smooth back for a minute, and then I stretched, long and slow, trying to shake off the bad dreams, my arms hitting the wooden headboard, my feet reaching toward the end of the bed . . .

And that's when I felt it.

Sand.

My hands went to my head, to my skin, to the sheets. It was everywhere. Crusted over my scalp, underneath my fingernails, underneath my pillow, caked around the necklace Neely gave me, in between my toes, everywhere.

I ran my fingertips down my cheek and sheets of it flaked off.

My hair was wet too; I felt it slap against my shoulder when I got up and started brushing at the quilt with my hands.

I was quiet, so quiet.

Slow, Vi, slow. Don't wake Neely.

My palms scraped the grit to the sandy floor, over and over, again and again.

Then I slipped off down the hall and got in the shower.

I didn't let myself think about it, not one thought, not for a second.

In the morning I would think it all a dream.

Chapter 12

June

I found her. And him. We had all come up from the city to celebrate Rose Redding's sixteenth birthday. Chester and Clara Glenship were her godparents, and she helped fill the hole that their poor broken-necked daughter Alexandra left when she fell from the tree house.

The sky on Rose's birthday was blue and clear. A perfect day for a perfect girl. She was apple-cheeked and chestnut-curled and innocent as one of the round brown puppies in the barn. I knew. I knew when Chase gave her that book of naughty French poetry for a present and she smiled up at him like he was God. I knew what he'd done.

Will figured it out later, when he found Rose in Chase's bed.

Chase was a fine match for me, in Will's mind. Daring, worldly, flashy Freddie. I could have handled him.

But not Rose.

Rose was the kind of girl to fall in love once, and forever. Chase and "forever" didn't mix.

I crawled into Will's arms that night, as I'd done so many nights before. I woke with a start, a few hours before dawn. Maybe I heard a scream. Or maybe not. Something called me to the cellar. I slid out from between Will's hands, and legs, and followed the feeling.

Chase was holding her, rocking back and forth, back and forth, her hair swinging between his elbows, blood soaking them both.

I saw the knife. Small. Steel. A red handle.

My heart broke. Right down the middle.

And the color went out of the world

≈≈≈

Canto was gone by the time we got up, off to fetch the fish, like she said. I read some of Freddie's diary in bed, and it was dark and sad. I sighed, got up, and brushed my teeth in the small bathroom down the hall—the water was hot enough but cut out when I still had toothpaste in my mouth. Living by the sea did bad things to pipes. I knew this from the Citizen. We'd had to abandon four of its seven bathrooms because nothing in them worked anymore.

I pulled on a clean wool skirt, tights, black boots, and a dark gray sweater. I saw a phone in the tower hallway, a black, metal one with a rotary dial. I wanted to call the Citizen, to see if Jack was all right, to see if Luke and Sunshine had made it home. I picked up the handset and put it to my ear . . . no dial tone. I guess Luke and I weren't the only kids who couldn't pay the phone bill sometimes.

Luke, are you all right?

I met Finch and Neely in the kitchen. Neely handed me a cup of espresso, and Finch gave me a red plate with a shiny poached egg wobbling to and fro on a piece of buttered toast.

"Never had them poached before," Finch said, and he seemed both amused and a bit scornful. "Only scrambled and fried and boiled. I guess this is how the city people eat their city eggs. They certainly take a lot more work."

But I caught a glimmer of a smile when Finch sliced through the egg and the orange-yellow yolk spilled out. He dipped a piece of toast into the yolk and took a bite. Another smile glimmer.

I looked between him and Neely while I ate, and enjoyed the view.

Finch didn't have freckles, like Jack, but his cheeks had a ruddy hue that matched his hair. He sat in a shaft of the morning sun, the sea in the background, the clean, fresh air making his red cheeks all the redder.

I turned to Neely.

Neely's clear, even skin and Kennedy-esque side-parted hair and strong jaw all said *I come from generations of blue blood–ery.* His laughing, fired-up blue eyes—they were all his own, though. And they were my favorite part. He smiled at me over his cup of coffee, and my cheeks went hot, damn it all to hell.

Canto still hadn't returned by the time we finished breakfast, so we decided to go into the little town and get some coffee, and the lay of the land. I wanted to see if any of the Carollie people were acting . . . strange. I wanted to know what we were up against. And Neely did too, based on the way his eyes went smart and dark when I suggested it.

We saw the horses again when we stepped out of Captain Nemo, only two of them, running and playing with each other, and it was a joy to watch. It really was.

I thought about the night before, Neely beside me, his warm calves heating up my cold toes, and the horses, and the wild, and the freedom, and the strange dreams I had, and all of it.

We walked down the main street and I found the coffee shop that I'd spotted the night before. A sign hung above the door that said *The Green Salmon*. We went in and let ourselves be caught up in the clamor of people needing joe. It was ten in the morning and all ages were present: kids still on their Christmas holiday and elderly people who had already been up for hours and fishermen in thick plaid shirts.

Carollie seemed like any nice small town with its own urban legend and café and hollering waves . . . except it was fresh and new and unexplored and clean-slated. And, therefore, exotic.

Until.

Until we were standing on Carollie's main street, breathing in the salty air, drinking the Green Salmon's special of the day, coconut milk lattes with cinnamon. We watched a small town go about its small-town life, batting our eyes against the bright sun. My gaze danced down the row of buildings, the little post office, the closed-for-the-season French restaurant, the chocolate store, the used bookstore, the knickknack store . . .

Nothing was wrong with this place. Not a thing. Canto had been meeting a boy in the night—probably one of those Greek god boys from the Hag's Shack. Perhaps she had to do it in secret because . . . because their fathers hated each other and were in the middle of a fishermen's feud with no chance to reconcile, and . . .

Finch saw it first. The poster on the telephone pole.

A boy.

A boy our age.

Missing.

He looked familiar. The dark hair, the tilt of his chin, the smile that went ear to ear . . .

I'd seen him. Recently.

Or someone who looked just like him.

Two brothers, both with the same hair and tilt and smiles . . .

A pretty woman in her early forties walked by. She caught us staring at the poster and stopped walking. She had long eyelashes and round shoulders and she held three sweet-looking greyhounds on a leash.

"Roman's been missing for weeks now," she said as her dogs rubbed their noses into our palms. "Some people are saying he ran off to the mainland, chasing a girl. He's one of the Finnfolk boys, fisher family, dark-eyed and rowdy, all of them, catching Carollie hearts as easily as they catch fish." The woman's face fell and she looked older all of a sudden. "Even the island crones go soft-eyed," she added, after a second, "whenever they catch sight of the Finnfolk boys hauling in the nets. And Roman there was the worst of the lot. Or the best, depending on your view . . ."

The woman trailed off. She wasn't looking at the poster anymore. She was looking at Canto, walking toward us, raven-haired and red-lipped and chipper in the morning sun.

"Hey, you three." Canto waved, smiled. "Fancy meeting you here. What are you all looking at?"

The woman turned, quick, and moved off down the street, her dogs loping behind.

Canto watched her go, her brow twisted up, smile gone.

None of us said anything. After all, boys went missing all the time, didn't they? Even rowdy, dark-eyed fisher boys with hearts on their sleeves.

Canto spun around, and saw the poster. She stared, blinked, and then turned her back to it. "What do you say we head home and get some work done?" she asked. She smiled again, but it was different this time. Stiff. Strained.

I opened my mouth to ask, saw the sharp look in her eyes, and shut it again.

Back at Captain Nemo, Neely helped Canto make more clam chowder and lemon crème fraiche sauce for the Hag's Shack. I cleaned things and dusted things and felt useful and wondered why the hell I didn't do this kind of thing back home, in the Citizen. Finch found a broom and swept sand into piles, and then swept those piles out into the sea.

A few hours later I finished cleaning. I stepped outside, onto one of Captain Nemo's worn decks. I breathed in the air, deep, deep, and then went down to the beach and sat in the cold sand and watched the waves. I thought about my parents and Jack and Luke and Sunshine and Freddie and Citizen Kane . . .

And Pine and Aggie and Inn's End and Finch . . .

And Neely and Brodie and River . . .

I got to my feet and started walking down the beach, going nowhere in particular.

It was faint at first. Just a whisper that seemed to float in on the waves.

Violet.

I stopped walking. I shut my eyes.

I heard it again. Closer.

Violet.

And the next time was right in my damn ear . . .

Violet . . .

. . . Like he was beside me, his body inches away, his lips on my neck . . .

I opened my eyes. Spun around.

There was nothing. No one. A long stretch of sand

without a single soul, silent except for the lapping of the waves at my toes.

River. He'd called out my name, plain as day. I'd heard it right over the roaring of the sea.

I shivered, hugged my chest, and waited for it to happen again.

But nothing.

I ran all the way back to Captain Nemo, the sea wind combing through my hair, sweeping in and out of my lungs. I went up the steps and inside and stood still in the doorway, catching my breath.

Quiet. Where was everyone? I called out names. No one answered.

The air was thick with the smell of the sea. Fish and sand and salt. It was overpowering suddenly, hovering like a cloud, clinging to my skin and my hair like I'd rolled in it, soaked it up, let it drench my pores.

Something about the smell, the lovely, familiar smell, felt odd to me.

Wrong.

Bad.

I went through the house, opening door after door, until I finally pushed through into a pipe-smoke-smelling study with a worn carpet and dark walls filled with water-warped books on fishing and sea-ing.

I turned, and there they were, in the far corner, in the shadows.

Canto's black curls meshing into Finch's straight red.

Her fingertips in his hair and her palms on his cheeks.

His body pressing into hers and his hands spread out across her lower back.

I didn't watch.

I only watched for a second.

Finch seemed to be holding back and Canto seemed to be pushing forward and it was personal, so personal. I backed out of the room and . . .

. . . and the next thing I knew I was sitting on Captain Nemo's front wooden deck, facing the great blue sea and trying to figure out why the hell I was crying. It was Neely who found me. He sat down and wrapped me up in his long arms until I didn't know where he ended and I began. His head was buried in my neck and he didn't laugh and he didn't talk. He didn't say one word until I was done.

"What happened?" he whispered. "What the hell happened?"

"I don't know," I said, because I didn't. "I stumbled onto Canto and Finch kissing in the study . . ."

"Canto and Finch? Already? That was fast," Neely said, and laughed.

And then I was laughing too, even though my cheeks

were still red from crying my damn eyes out for no reason.

"I'm not a crier," I said. "This doesn't make me a crier."

Neely nodded. "I know."

We both just sat and listened to the sea roar out its feelings for a while.

"I think I'm going mad," I said, after a bit. "Neely, how do you know if you're going mad?"

Neely raised his eyebrows at me. "People like you don't go mad, Vi. They're quiet on the outside and loud on the inside and sane as the day is long."

I shook my head. "I went for a walk on the beach and I heard River say my name. Three times. Clear as a bell, as if he were standing right next to me. How the hell do you explain this?"

Neely shrugged. "The sea will make you hear all sorts of things. It's tricksy and spiteful." He put his hand to his ear, and leaned forward. "Right now the waves are telling *me* to take off all my clothes and tap-dance down the shore. See? That's not good advice. I'm not doing that." He put his hand back down. "As I said, tricksy and spiteful."

I laughed.

And then Neely cupped my head with his hand and I tilted right back into his palm, chin in the air, natural as breathing. And when he brought his face down, down toward mine, my insides went soaring up, up . . .

His lips touched mine, light and soft as snowflakes melting on my skin . . .

I closed my eyes . . .

. . . and started hearing the sea, louder now, like I was in it, under it, the bellow and the blast and the tides and the crash . . .

Neely's fingers slipped from my hair.

I opened my eyes.

Cornelius Redding was on his feet, looking down on me, his blues meeting mine. "I'm so sorry, Vi," was all he said.

And then he just walked back inside. And I was alone.

≈

Neely and me never did get to the Lillian Hut. Night fell fast and we all went along with Canto to help feed the Hag's Shack crowd. We met her regulars and everyone was cheerful and easy to talk to. It felt like we'd been on the island for months, not hours.

"I could live here," Finch said, decisive and brooking no refusal. We were walking back to the rambling Nemo after shutting up shop. Finch and Canto walked side by side, the wind whipping their clothes about their bodies and their hair about their faces. "I like being able to see. The forest was dark. Close. I'm done with it, for now. I like the openness of this island. I like seeing forever."

Canto looked up into his face, and he looked down into hers, and suddenly they were looking at each other, deep, like they were all alone, and Canto's eyes were alert and dark and her face said *You'll do, forest boy,* and Finch's face said *I didn't know how much I needed this,* and he looked kind of happy and mysterious underneath the caged and wild.

Neely's hand slipped into mine and I let it. Back and forth with him, back and forth. I held his hand tight under a sky full of stars and understood everything about him, right then.

That night by the fire I told Canto about Citizen Kane, and Luke, and Sunshine, and Jack, and my parents. She asked interested questions about art and Echo, and the conversation flowed like the hot caramel milk we couldn't stop drinking.

Canto talked about her seafaring father, and she seemed to idolize him and loathe him at the same time. She thought he had another family, somewhere in the South Pacific maybe, but she didn't have proof. Yet. She said that Captain Nemo had a ghost, a curly-haired boy who was killed in a storm at the turn of the century. She said she was a casual prophet, and that the prophesizing blood came from her mother's side. She said she'd dreamed of Finch and recognized him the first night we arrived. And we listened and laughed and believed some of it and not the rest.

She didn't talk about the boy on the poster. The Finnfolk boy. Roman. And I didn't ask.

River, I don't want this to end. Any of it, anything that has started here in another house on the sea with a red-haired orphan and a complicated, missing-parent girl and one Violet White and one Redding boy.

CHAPTER 13

I WAS RUNNING across the beach again, feet sinking into the wet sand.

I looked over my shoulder at Captain Nemo, nothing but one long, angular shadow reaching into the dark velvet sky. Finch was standing on the top deck, pale face and red hair and moonlight streaming down behind him. He was watching me. But he didn't wave, or call out, so neither did I. I kept running.

Running.

Running.

I saw it.

The Lillian Hut.

Small. Tattered. Little square windows. Peeling paint. Long wooden deck. Pointed roof. Stilts in the sand.

Something pitch-black beat its wings against the dark sky. A raven. It flew down and landed on the edge of the roof.

Silence, except for the sea and the cawing of the big black bird.

My wrists hurt. The harsh sea wind bit at my tender, scarred skin. I tugged my sleeves down.

I climbed the rotting steps.

Rusted knob.

Weather-beaten door.

I went in.

And there he was. Sleeping on a pile of nets in the corner, one naked arm thrown over his head. His eyes were closed and his expression was soft and moonlight was shooting through one of the windows and he looked like a damn angel, a damn Titian angel.

I'd found him.

I'd found River.

After all that, after all the wondering and worrying and Devil hunting, here he was.

He was thin. So thin. Lean muscles, taut and tense like they were about to snap. Long dirty hair, down to his chin. Expensive linen pants, torn and ragged and tied with a rope around his waist and still hanging half off his skinny body. No shirt in the cold. Nothing from the waist up.

No shoes. Black dirt under his fingernails. White, sea-salt crust on his skin.

I took a deep breath.

The room smelled like fish and salty sea air.

I turned my head.

Rods and reels and other fishing things. Old nets and dried seaweed. A small wooden table with black grime ground into its cracks. A short, dirty knife next to a pile of oyster shells and one small cup filled with dirty water.

This, this was how River was living.

River, who made sweet-potato fries and eggs in a frame and bought expensive dark chocolate. River, who needed espresso six times a day and hated thunderstorms but loved *Casablanca* and whose skin and hair had always smelled so clean, like fresh cold air.

Rustling in the corner.

River's eyes were open.

"Hi, Violet," he said. Just like that. Just like it was nothing.

"Hi, River," I said.

He sat up. He gestured to the pile of nets beneath him. "Very different from the old days, back in the snug guesthouse, huh, Vi? I haven't been sleeping very well lately."

"You have nightmares," I whispered.

He nodded. "I have nightmares." He paused. "Vi, do

you remember when you used to crawl in bed next to me? You kept the nightmares away. Do you remember?"

"I do."

He smiled the crooked smile at me.

And suddenly he didn't look thin and gaunt and rangy anymore. He was sleek and svelte and sinewy like the very first day I saw him, walking up to the steps of Citizen Kane.

My heart filled.

Sizzling, steaming, blood-red joy.

"River, we've been so worried," I said, words as fast as my beating heart. "We thought you teamed up with Brodie . . . we thought you were a devil-boy in Virginia . . . we thought you were a sea god . . ."

River was on his feet now. His arms went around me and my arms went around him. My eyes closed and my face pressed into his neck. I smelled salt and fish and sea, though. Not River. Not leaves and autumn and midnight.

He kissed me. Thumb under my chin, his lips separating mine, my head tilting back, his hands underneath my sweater, and down the front of my wool skirt, and my fingertips dragging across his naked back, and the nails filling with salt, and my mind went blank, and I wanted to die with joy, and I wanted to live forever, and I heard nothing, nothing but water hitting rocks, and ships hitting ice, and whales singing, and someone drowning, and I was starting to drown too, sink down, below the waves, give up my breath, let it go, go, go, down to the deep, down past the horses, down where I couldn't see the kicking and the swinging, down in the black . . .

River leaned into my ear and whispered something. Something I knew was important, very important. But I couldn't hear his voice over the roaring, spitting sea, couldn't hear it at all—

"Violet, are you awake?"

Neely.

I blinked my eyes. Opened them. I was sitting on the window seat, knees tucked under my chin, cheek against the cold, slick glass. I'd fallen asleep here, waiting for him. I'd been having another nightmare. Another River nightmare. I was shivering, covered in goose bumps, and my hands were ice—I put them to my head and my hair was in wet strings and my skin was coated with sand. I jumped off the window seat and grabbed a towel and began to rub and squeeze and try to get it all, get it all off.

I was going mad

I took a deep breath, and brushed the last bit of sand from the back of my neck.

After we followed Canto, and found out where she was going, we would come back here and Neely would crawl in my bed again and then I'd tell him about the sand and the dreams.

And he would make it stop.

It was just a glow thing, a leftover glow thing. Neely would understand.

"Violet?"

My door opened.

I stood and turned and he was already halfway across the room.

He put his hand on my chest. Right in the middle. Fingers spread wide. He guided me back, gently, until my body touched the wall between the windows and the dresser.

I closed my eyes and pictured the wild horses.

River's brother kissed me in the darkest hour of the night at the darkest time of the year, but what I felt when his lips touched mine wasn't darkness.

It was clear warm bursts of yellow high noon sunshine.

I kissed him back.

I let that sunshine pour right over me, right through me. I ran to meet it.

Neely pulled away, and laughed, a whooping, happy, Neely-laugh.

"I had to do it," he said. "In case something happens tonight. In case we find something. I had to do it, Vi."

Then he was kissing me again, up my cheeks and down

my neck and under my necklace and over my shoulders and inside my elbows and back up my arms and I could feel his hip bones through my nightgown and I could feel my heart beating and my skin tingling and my thoughts tingling and I was wide-wake and wide-eyed and it was everything, everything.

Neely drained the last lingering glow right out of me with those kisses.

What I'd had with River last summer didn't seem wonderful anymore.

It didn't seem mysterious and exciting and beautiful.

It felt wrong. *Wrong.* Wrong, wrong, wrong.

Wrong like plagues of locusts and seas of blood and death of the firstborn and hail, thunder, darkness.

Neely whispered *sorry, sorry* in between the kisses, but I didn't know if he was saying it to me or to River . . . and then I was crying again, though I didn't know why because I was so damn happy, I was about to burst out of my skin, and Neely brushed the tears off my face with his thumb. He kissed me, and I kissed him back, on and on, and the tears ran down my cheeks, though I didn't understand them and didn't want them there, and they slipped down my neck, damp and warm and unwelcome.

"I'm not a crier," I said, eventually. Though I guess I was now.

“I know, Vi, I know.” Neely’s lips went to the soft spot behind my left ear. “I’ve wanted to kiss you since the first second I saw you,” he whispered, “since the first second I saw you curled up in my brother’s arms.”

I put my hands on Neely’s face, and tilted it down to mine. Then I lifted my wet eyes to his, and looked deep.

I saw his temper, jumping about and stamping its feet and waiting for a chance to shine.

I saw the glint that all the Redding brothers shared, the I’m-going-to-glow-or-fight-or-whatever-I-want-and-no-one-will-stop-me-not-even-you glint.

But I also saw something else . . . something that made my damn heart screech to a halt.

Something that had been there all along, I think.

I heard the front door open and close. I sighed, and dropped my hands.

I walked to the bay window and looked down. A flashlight turned on and a beam of light started moving away from the house.

Neely breathed in. And let it out.

I watched the light . . .

And I felt dread start to fill me up, black and loud as the sea.

But I felt the restless itch begin to surge back too.

My feet wanted to move, run, kick up sand, go, go, go . . .

CHAPTER 14

FINCH CAUGHT US on the steps. He'd woken up when he heard Canto's bedroom door open and so he was coming too, damn it.

We followed the beam of Canto's flashlight. We walked across Captain Nemo's main deck, our feet crunching in the sand. Down the steps. Down to the beach.

Within seconds Canto got too far ahead and then all I could see was the light, bobbing and bouncing ahead of us, leading us on.

We walked for a mile, maybe more. Finch was quiet. Neely was quiet. I was quiet. The sea was not. There was a storm out on the ocean somewhere and the water was slapping the sand and the wind was yelling in our ears.

I looked at Neely, stretching up tall into the dark sky,

the ocean gales whipping his shirt open at the neck so I could see the top of his scar, faint in the moonlight.

The sand curved around a hill and opened into a hidden little cove.

Our beam of light joined the others. Dozens of yellow lights, blinding us.

We sank down behind the tall grass that bordered the inlet, sheltered from the wind, but I could still hear it howling at the edges, trying to get in.

The flashlights clicked off just as the moon came out from behind the clouds.

I saw them all.

The people drinking coconut milk lattes in the Green Salmon. The greyhound woman. The regulars at the Hag's Shack. Kids, the elderly, everyone. The sea wind spun their hair and their clothes and everything fluttered and flapped, and their eyes were closed but their mouths were open, slack round circles . . .

And, right smack in the middle, was Canto.

Finch made a sound when he saw her, a low moan in the back of his throat like winter wind whistling through dead winter trees. But he didn't go to her, didn't shout her name.

I saw a fisherman's hut off to my right.

And I flinched at the sight of it.

There was something . . .

Some idea, some memory . . .

I'd seen that hut before . . .

I'd been *in* that hut before . . .

Some of the islanders began to gather driftwood into a pile. Others squatted next to black buckets and began to clean the fish in them with sharp knives. Some held children. Some just stood still, still as death, arms at their sides, staring at the sea like it was the answer to their prayers.

They didn't move like real people. They moved like . . . sleepwalkers. Luke used to sleepwalk, when he was a kid. I remembered the sound of his somnambulist feet in the hallway, shuffling, hesitant, ungraceful, unnatural. I would throw back my covers and find him standing outside my door, eyes wide open and unseeing. I'd grab his arm and shake him, over and over, until he woke up with a start, until he said something like *What the hell is your problem, Vi?* before turning around and going back to bed.

I thought about Jack's father, Daniel Leap, stumbling into the town square, moving like the people in front of me, and not from the drink for once. I thought about my grandfather Lucas breaking his arm when he fell down the stairs, and the priest, burning up the church with himself inside, and Rose Redding, her life pouring out through the slit in her neck . . .

And suddenly I couldn't breathe, couldn't remember how to do it. I stuck my chest out and sucked my stomach in and nothing happened, and it was like drowning. I was drowning fifty feet from the sea.

And then Finch was wrapping me in his tough forest arms, pressing my face into his shoulder until the grass tickled my neck. He held me hard until the breath came. In and out. In and out.

Neely glanced at me in Finch's arms, but then went right back to watching the islanders. They had dropped what they were doing now and were forming a semicircle around the fisherman's hut. We watched as they stood, silent, arms at their sides. My breath went in and out, in and out. The islanders fell to their knees, eyes lowered. Even the children kneeled, short legs bent beneath them, small heads tilted down.

I heard a noise in the hut. An about-to-open-the door noise.

Neely's hands were twitching. I could see them in the moonlight, rattling the nearby blades of grass.

We got to our feet . . .

Just as a naked-from-the-waist-up William Redding III stepped out of the hut.

It was him.

It was.

It was River.

It flooded through me like full tide, like the sea singing in my ears . . . the dirty shack, River sleeping like an angel, like a damn angel, River's hands on me, skin to skin, and more, and more, and more, and the heat, and the cold, and the pulse, and the wanting and River's whisper, right in my ear, *Don't remember, Vi, don't see me like this, leave here, don't remember . . .*

The sand, and the dreams, and the crying, and Neely . . .

Oh, Neely . . .

I felt a scream building in the back of my throat, getting stronger . . . growing teeth . . . claws . . .

Don't think about it, Vi, don't think about it, there's no time, not now, you'll go mad, don't think about it—

The islanders' heads were lowered, and River's was raised to the sky. He stretched his arms out, palms up. He opened his mouth. Sounds came out . . . but no words. At least, not words I understood.

Like Alice, like *'twas brillig and the slithy toves* . . . River's words almost made sense. Maybe if I listened close enough, I would understand. I could almost . . . I was so close . . .

The islanders, eyes shut, knees still kissing the sand, joined him.

"They're praying to River," Neely said. His eyes were fixed on his brother, standing there on the hut's deck, half naked, arms in the air. "And River is praying to the sea." Neely breathed in deep, and sighed.

River's voice surrounded us, louder now that the crowd had joined in. It sounded like the sea, like creaking boards and cold winds from the north and captains going down with the ship and fins fluttering in the dark and . . .

Finch's shoulder touched mine, and a second later, Neely's. They sandwiched me between them, side by side.

I opened my eyes.

"Be careful, Vi," Finch said, his fingers weaving into mine, squeezing tight.

River stopped the sea words, snap, as quick as he'd started, and the islanders went silent, snap, just as fast, and Finch's last two words rang out into the new, brittle silence.

River lowered his arms.

The islanders stood up. They didn't see us, didn't hear us, didn't look at us. A group of them broke off and lit the driftwood. A fire blazed up.

River always did like his bonfires.

I saw Canto. Her dress swished against her legs as she shuffled to the side of the hut and crouched down in the sand.

River turned around then, away from the sea.

He looked straight at the three of us standing in the tall grass at the edge of the cove. Like he knew we'd been there all along.

His eyes perked up. I swear they did.

And then he smiled his crooked smile like it was all nothing. Like he was right where he wanted to be, beautiful and lean in the December cold, the world at his feet.

Nothing had changed. Nothing had changed at all.

"Hey, Violet," he said.

Espresso and olive oil and tomatoes and midnight and kids in cemeteries and sizzling, crackling fear and a blood-dripping neck and fire and smoke and the warm, happy feeling of the glow flowing through me and through him, buzz and hum and purr and kissing in the guesthouse and the shack with the dirt and the nets and the seaweed and the salt under my fingernails and River's hands pulling at my clothes . . .

"Violet," River repeated. "Would you like to join me while my congregation prepares a sea feast?"

I stepped out into the full light of the newly built fire. The Carollians ignored me. There were no flashes of recognition, no looks, no waves, no nothing. Not even from Canto. She was sitting cross-legged in the sand, head bent, shucking oysters. Finch and Neely followed me. Finch called out her name as we walked past, voice soft and urgent, but her eyes, when she looked at him, weren't alert and scrappy. They were big and black and dead. Dead like Gianni's had been, up in the Glenship attic before he tried to set Jack on fire. Dead like Cassie's and Sam's had been, after beating their daughter, Sunshine.

The three of us walked up the two steps to the long deck that circled the old fisherman's hut. River smiled his lazy smile and moved aside to let us through the door.

I didn't meet his eyes as I passed.

If he smiled at me in that crooked way again . . .

I'd lose my mind.

Maybe I already had.

I heard the sea sounds again in my head, like before, River whispering, singing—singing me down to the deep, *with the whales and the fish and the sunken ships and the mermaids and the eels and the half-human seals . . .*

My eyes closed . . .

Finch yanked me through the doorway and into the room. Neely put his hands on my shoulders, and shook me gently until my head bobbed up and down. "Stop it, Vi," he whispered. "Don't let him in. Stop it."

"How?" I stared at Neely. And then I turned and looked around the dank, murky room. "I think . . . I think I've been here before . . . the sand in the bed . . . and my hair all wet, I—"

River shut the red door behind him, and the sound of the sea softened. He swept his right arm through the air. "It's not much, just a humble fisherman's shack, but what's more fitting for a sea king? We have the ocean, and our people. You may sit." He motioned toward four overturned crates under two small, dirty windows.

The only light in the hut came from a half-dead candle on the table and the bonfire outside the small square windows. I sat down on a crate by Neely and Finch. I was shaking. I tilted my head back and looked River full in the face for the first time.

His eyes had changed. Even in the gloom, I could see it. They were brown still, shiny deep brown, but that mysterious, mischief-loving glint from before . . . it was gone.

Now River's eyes were just . . .

Wrong.

Off. Jittery. Bad.

"And who is this before us?" River asked, looking at Finch. "Is it our brother Brodie? He had red hair. We seem to remember him having red hair." River still stood by the door, shoulders straight, eyes narrowed.

"Not Brodie. Finch. Finch Grieve." Finch's expression was calm, calm and caged and not wild, not wild at all.

"So you're calling yourself a sea king." Neely's voice

sounded strange. Wound up tight and ready to spring. It was so un-Neely, so un-Neely of an hour ago, up in the treasure map room, it made my ears ache to hear it. "We heard about a sea *god*," Neely added, shrugging, "but a sea king is just as good, isn't it, River?"

"Sea king," River repeated, low and soft and sly. "Yes. King of the barnacle. King of the algae, the abalone, the sea horse, the sand dollar, the eel, the mollusk, the brine." River leaned his naked torso against the wall by the door and crossed his arms. "Who are you again?" he asked, looking at me. "Come over here so we can get a good look at you."

I jerked to my feet.

Neely snapped his arm out and blocked my way. "Don't let him touch you."

River's eyes cleared for a moment, like mist evaporating in the sun. He looked right at Neely, and smiled. "Oh, that. That's all over. The sea has made us strong. It took us and gave us back. We were drowned and then un-drowned. We were remade in the sea king's image. Skin on skin became a thing of the past. The glow, the burn, the spark, it flows right from us to these simple islanders now, flowing, flowing, like the water and the tides, never stopping, on and on and on—"

Neely's fists clenched at his sides, and the muscles in

his neck went tight. "Stop it, River. Simple islanders? Sea king? I can't keep listening to this—"

"You," River said, ignoring Neely and looking at me. He tilted his head and pointed a finger at my face. "I think I almost loved you once."

I shook my head. "No, you never did," I said. "You never did."

River raised his eyebrows. "Or maybe it wasn't you. I loved a blond-haired girl by the sea, though, once upon a time. It was *many and many a year ago, in a kingdom by the sea, that Annabel Lee lived with no other thought than to love and be loved by me.*"

River paused. "No, that's not right. Annabel belonged to someone else. You're Violet. And I did love you once. I did. I think I did."

Neely's cheeks had gone red, and the red was bleeding down his neck.

If Neely hit River . . .

River would kill him.

"Kiss me, Violet or girl-who-reminds-me-of-Violet," River said. "Come here and kiss me."

I looked at Neely. He was breathing fast, and his hands were twitching.

"It might break his madness," I said. "It might bring him back, Neely."

I don't know why the hell I thought this. I just did. Something about this hut—I remembered . . . I had kissed him in here, and it had helped . . .

Hadn't it?

"Don't do it. Don't you do it." Neely's voice was low and hot and wired.

Was he talking to me, or River?

Did I care?

River . . . before . . . in the shack . . . he'd been skinny and dirty and in bad shape, but he had still been River. But this sea king boy before me . . . He was a stranger.

I went to him anyway.

He needed me.

River needed me.

I let him slide his dirty sea king hands into my hair. He gripped my skull. Tight.

I forgot Finch. I forgot Neely.

It's summer and you're standing in the guesthouse kitchen and the smell of coffee lingers in the air and his heart is pressed into yours and his fingers are slipping down your skin and it's already gone too far and not far enough and you don't want it to stop . . .

His lips parted like the sea.

I thought of Freddie and Will and Will's burning and Rose's swinging hair and the blood soaking them both . . .

River, River, I don't care what you've done, I don't care how mad you are, it's not your fault, it's not your fault . . .

I tasted salt and madness and it was River River River familiar and it tasted so damn good I wanted to drown in it, let the water steal my breath, fill my lungs, jerk, sigh, darkness, limp, floating away.

CHAPTER 15

"VIOLET."

River pulled back and I stared up at him. His eyes were changing. I could see it, like watching the sun sweep the clouds away, leaving a blue sky behind.

I'd kissed him and brought him back. River was Sleeping Beauty and I was the prince and fairy tale, fairy tale. My heart started to swell, soar, and I thought, *I've done it, I saved him, it will be like before, like last summer, and we'll find Brodie, and fight him, and we'll win this time . . .*

I turned and looked at Neely. His fists were clenched, his cheeks red, and his eyes were sad, and lost, and angry, and hopeful, and full of wanting, wanting, wanting . . .

Then River shook his head and the clouds came snapping back. His eyes drifted to the pile of nets in the corner, and mine followed.

"Sleep next to me tonight, Vi," River said. "Let's send these two away and lie down in the nets and kiss and sleep and dream."

I shook my head. "No, River. I can't, I don't . . ."

I closed my eyes.

I heard the sea.

The waves beat out a pattern and my heart echoed it back, and I was sinking, sinking into the deep again, the deep, deep, deep . . .

"Violet," Finch said, loudly.

I opened my eyes. Rubbed them. They felt gritty, jagged, scratched, like my face had been buried in sand.

River was still staring at me.

"Stay with me here, Vi," River said, again. He reached out and pulled me back into him. His mouth went to my ear. "I need you to sleep with me on my nets and keep the nightmares away. I can't let them"—he flicked his hand toward the window, at the people outside—"I can't let them know about the nightmares. They won't understand. But you understand."

"I don't," I said, shaking my head.

"You do," River answered.

"She *doesn't,*" Neely said. He took two steps forward.

And then one step back.

I knew what that was like. I'd been there.

I was there now.

"Violet, be my sea queen," River sang into my ear, soft and whispery. "Stay with me here, under the sea. We'll grow gills like the fish, and swim from coast to coast, pole to pole, our people following behind. And each night *I will strip you of your seaweed clothes and kiss your scales and stroke your tails and . . .*"

River whispered on and on. I began to watch the islanders outside the window as his voice droned in my ear. They had joined together and formed a circle around the fire. Their voices rose. Their legs moved. Their arms. Necks, bellies. A strange, swelling sea dance. Their voices got louder, their bodies undulating, bending, flopping, tossing, faster, faster, swirling around the fire, arms, legs, hair, elbows, hands, knees, feet, merging into a single slumping, curving mass, in a way that made my heart feel sick and twisted with the wrongness of it—

River stopped talking. His hands dropped from my body. He turned around and looked out the window. "Ah," he said, in a quiet, knowing sort of way.

He stepped lightly over the fishing nets on the floor and opened the door of the hut and went outside. A cold burst of wind hit us and my hair lifted straight up. Finch was watching me and River, but Neely had his back turned to all of us. I pulled my cardigan closer and went up behind him and put my arms around him. He grabbed my hands and squeezed me back. And then we all followed River out onto the hut's deck.

"They are calling for the sacrifice," River said. "The sea demands we sacrifice a virgin before each full moon sea feast. Stay here—this won't take long." River put out a thin arm and pointed at a dark-haired girl whose flopping body was dancing by. "You, you'll do."

The girl stopped. She stepped out of the circle, and came toward River.

It was Canto.

River walked down the steps to the sand. He put his dirty sea king hands in her curly black hair, and then he kissed her. Deep. Slow. Soft. Like twilight disappearing into night.

The islanders stopped dancing, and watched.

Canto's hands went to River's naked back, and gripped tight.

Finch, Neely, me, none of us moved. We didn't stop it. We didn't do anything. And maybe we were stunned, or maybe River was glowing us up, who knows.

River's fingers slid down Canto's arms. He took both of her hands.

"What's your name?" he asked her, loud enough so we could hear him above the waves.

"Canto," she said. And her eyes were black and empty, but her lips were wet and red.

"Canto, we need you to sacrifice yourself to the sea. You will drink the water and let it fill your lungs. You will sink into the deep and become the sea's lover. After you cross into the sea world, we will give you our breath, and try to bring you back. The sea may keep you . . . or she may reject you. It's up to her. Do you understand?"

Canto nodded. And River pulled her forward, step by step into the water. They walked into the frigid ocean until it was lapping at Canto's thighs, her skirt lifting up with the waves.

The islanders stretched out across the sand, watching, not moving, not talking.

Except for the three boys.

They came up behind Neely and Finch and me right as River was kissing Canto.

They wrapped us in their strong arms . . .

And squeezed.

And squeezed.

Finch struggled and shouted and Neely struggled and shouted and I pounded my elbows into the thick torso behind me and it made no difference, not a bit of difference.

River said something I couldn't hear and Canto fell to her knees. The sea was sloshing near her throat now, her curly hair going straight in the water and fanning out on all sides.

Finch was still yelling next to me, and Neely was screaming River's name and the wind was howling and I could smell the ocean on the boy behind me, feel his scruffy chin scratch the top of my ear.

River wouldn't drown her, he couldn't . . .

But then he looked up, right at me, and the look on his face was eager and his eyes had gone wrong again and then he was pressing his right palm into Canto's face, fingers outstretched, and pushing her backward into the waves . . .

Finch broke free. He burst out of the islander's arms and started running. Water splashed out from his body in great dark arcs.

"*Take me instead,*" Finch screamed out against the pound pound pound.

River turned his head toward Finch, and stared at him.

Tick-tock, tick-tock, Canto was still pushed underwater.

Slowly, slowly, River's hand rose.

Canto's head popped back out of the sea. Her black hair was thick and streaming and she coughed and coughed.

She opened her eyes and they were empty still, blank and black and horrid.

She got to her feet and staggered back to the beach and threw herself on the sand, her body still half in the water. I wanted to go to her and grab her in my arms—

But the boy held me tight so tight against him and nothing I did made any difference.

"Finch," I begged, calling out across the water. "Don't. *Don't.*"

Finch kept moving, toward River.

Not *Finch*. I *saved* him, we saved him, Neely and me—

River's posture was kingly and bored, and his thin body stood firm against the waves. He looked at me. And he smiled.

"Don't worry, Vi. We will bring him back," River shouted. "The sea won't want him. We can always tell. We will bring him back, like we have before."

I might have started screaming again then, but maybe it was just the ocean in my ears. Finch kneeled in the water and River pushed him under and—

Neely hit River, fist to face, hard, cracking, smacking hard. One second he was struggling with the islander and the next he was in the water, fists flying. River's head snapped to the side. Neely hit him again, this time in the stomach, and the sea swirled around them both . . .

River waved his hand in the air like he was swatting a fly, and Neely started screaming. He dropped his arm, mid-hit, and spun in circles, seeing something in the sky that made him scream and duck and scream. I strained against the boy behind me, strained and pulled and my neck went taut, so taut my spine ached down my back and the boy was built of stone and didn't budge, not an inch, so I turned my head and screamed into his shoulder and I saw that he was dark-eyed and wild-looking and beautiful and I knew he was a Finnfolk boy, I just knew.

It only took a few minutes. A few minutes of Finch's flailing body before he went still.

Neely stopped yelling and started rubbing his eyes.

The Finnfolk boy let me go.

I ran to Canto. My black boots filled with water and my skirt went heavy with it and stuck to my legs, and I felt cold cold wet on my calves and my knees, so cold it burned. Empty-eyed Canto clung to me and I let her. The water slapped our sides and made us rock and stagger. I was shivering with cold now, and my feet felt heavy and dead and no longer mine, and Canto was shivering too, great big shivers, and I saw something flash in her empty eyes, just for a second, something dark and scared and so, so sad, but then it was gone just as fast.

I helped Canto to the beach, and then let go of her,

gentle, gentle. She sank to the ground, cheek to sand.

River carried Finch to the shore. He was stronger than he looked, and he made it seem easy, holding Finch's limp body high above the water as he waded in. He laid Finch down, next to Canto.

The moon disappeared behind a cloud and everything went dark and Finch's red hair was slick and black and it stuck to his face, his lips, his nose, everywhere, and his skin was cold and hard and glistening in the shadowy bonfire light and it made him seem narrow and different, blue and cold and gaunt and not like himself at all. River started pumping his chest, pump, pump, pump, and then breathing in his mouth. Over and over. Over and over.

It's going to work, I thought, *it's going to work. It has to.*

After a few seconds Neely shoved River out of the way and took over. Pump, breathe, pump, breathe.

He's going to choke and spit up water, any second now, he is, he is.

I shouted at River, horrible, horrible things, and he just stood off to the side and looked bored.

Behind us the islanders started rubbing their eyes. They gave a sort of twitch, and then turned and started wandering back into the town.

Neely pumped and breathed and nothing, nothing.

River looked up at the sky, and then back down at Neely.

He yawned. "Well, it doesn't work every time. I guess the sea wanted him after all."

I bent down and picked up a piece of driftwood. It was gray and heavy and the size of Finch's forearm.

I knew the spot. Luke had hit me there once when we were little. He thought he killed me and maybe he almost had.

Neely gave up at last and pounded his fists on the sand.

Canto shook herself and got up and started walking back to Captain Nemo without a word.

River's face loomed in front of me, dark wet hair, shiny brown eyes, bored, bored, bored—

The end of the driftwood hit his jaw.

I had kissed that pretty jaw once upon a time. Slow, gentle kisses. Dark-of-night kisses. I had kissed that jaw in River's bed, with River's body pressed up into mine.

River twisted. Crumpled.

The sea king hit the sand.

And then Finch opened his eyes, and began coughing up the sea.

CHAPTER 16

December

Rose was dead and buried, and Chase locked up with the mad.

Chester and Clara Glenship left town and didn't come back.

I was a White now. I married Lucas in June. A week after Rose was murdered. Three months before Chase went to trial and was declared insane and committed to the state asylum. Four months before the world crashed and men jumped from tall buildings, and fortunes ebbed and flowed like the tide.

Lucas put all his money in gold, and survived.

I almost pushed Will over, the last time we

stood on the cliffs, looking at the ocean. I had my palms to his back . . .

But he guessed what I was about to do and turned and grabbed me to him and kissed me until I couldn't see straight.

It's Will who should be in there. In the madhouse. Not Chase.

Will.

And me.

≈≈≈

Captain Nemo.

River knocked out and sprawled across the middle of the floor, his starved arms limp at his sides.

Finch by the fire, naked and shivering under a quilt like he'd never get warm again, dark circles under his eyes, teeth chattering between pale lips, the flames casting strange shadows on his skin.

Canto sitting on the sofa and staring at the wall with her eyes still blank and hollow.

Neely, hair wet, crouched over his brother, looking lost and sad and scared and angry and relieved.

I sat down next to Finch and took his hand in mine.

I knew what it was like to be half killed by a Redding brother.

≈≈≈

Dawn. I'd fallen asleep on the living room floor, next to the fire, buried under a pile of blankets with Finch next to me. River was either sleeping or still out cold and Neely was beside him. Who knew where Canto was. Out getting the fish maybe.

She probably remembered nothing. She probably woke up in her own bed and walked downstairs and through the living room and wondered why we were all sleeping on the floor and who the hell the tied-up new boy was, before she stepped over him on her way out the door.

Yes, I had tied River's hands and feet before I went to sleep. Even though Neely had told me this alone wouldn't stop him from using the glow, if he wanted to. Even though I knew that as well as him.

I threw off two patchwork quilts, got up, and bent over the two Redding boys. Neely was smiling in his sleep, his arm thrown over his head and his quilts pushed down and his shirt riding halfway up his long, smooth torso.

And River. He looked so pale, so still. I put my hand on his chest to see if he was breathing. My palm touched his ribs, and his eyes shot open. His fingers snapped around my wrist.

"We need to get off the island, Vi," he whispered, voice still cracked and raw from yelling against the sea the night before. "They . . . I'm too . . . my head hurts too much. I won't be able to keep up the glow. People will start remembering. They'll come looking for me. For us. Help me, Vi. We need to go." His fingers squeezed against my scar and made it ache.

Someone knocked on the front door and I jerked. River let go of my wrist. Neely's eyes opened and River's closed again.

Neely got up without saying a word and went to the window to see who it was. I followed.

Hayden. Standing in the sun and holding a pail of oysters in one hand, the wild horses running down the beach behind him.

I didn't know how Hayden knew we needed to leave, but he did.

I slipped my fingers between Neely's and kept staring out the window. "We have to get back to the mainland," I whispered. "River thinks the islanders are going to start remembering soon."

Neely sighed. Nodded.

He opened the front door and let Hayden in.

We hustled and bustled and stuck River in a hot shower and got him dressed and he let us, weak as he was. Canto came back as we were packing and Finch pulled her aside and whispered something in her ear that made her eyes twinkle and flash and then she was throwing clothes in a ragged blue suitcase. We whispered good-byes to Captain Nemo and then slunk off down the beach to Hayden's boat. We didn't look any of the Carollie fishermen in the eye on the way, not one.

The wild horses lined up on the shore and tossed their heads and watched our boat take off, almost as if they were saying good-bye.

Neely took River to the small living space below deck. River was dizzy and sick and I suppose he had a concussion from my hitting him with the driftwood. But his injury was keeping him calm and seemed to be stopping him from using his glow for the time being, so I can't say I gave a damn.

He'd glowed me up in that shack, made me forget him, left me smelling like sea and sand and feeling a hole in my heart and not knowing why.

He'd killed Finch. Drowned him. Right in front of me.

It wasn't just Neely and me that were in danger now. We'd involved Finch and Canto in this Devil mess too.

Canto was on the other end of the boat, watching her island disappear into the morning mist. I wondered how long it had been since she'd left Carollie. I wondered if she left her father a note about where she was going, or if she didn't even bother.

I stood beside Finch, looking over the moving water,

my hip almost touching his. His eyes were distant and his expression was detached. Calm. He didn't look like someone who'd just been cradled in Death's arms . . . someone who'd stared down the dark beyond and then was resurrected when it seemed too late. He just looked like . . . Finch.

Except for the hair. His hair seemed less red now. It was dull and flat, like the water had sucked the color out of him as it had sucked out his life.

"I wonder if I left a part of me, down there, when I died," Finch said. We both stared at the slipping, sliding water. "I wonder if part of me is trapped, walking the seabed like a ghost." He paused. "Just like a part of me is still in the woods back home, haunting my small bit of the forest."

"Why did you do it?" I asked, voice quiet, almost a whisper. "Why did you take Canto's place last night?"

Finch turned to me, and his eyes had that wild look again. "Death came for me in Inn's End," he said. "And I escaped him. But I . . . I have this feeling that he's never going to stop looking for me, never going to stop biting at my heels. I thought I might as well meet him halfway, on my own terms, and see who's the better man."

The sea wind lifted his faded red hair and swirled it about his head, as if it agreed.

"That," he added, "and the fact that I'm falling in love with Canto." He smiled, and it was shy and forest-boy and savage and primal all at the same time. He looked over my shoulder at the curly-haired island girl, and then back at me, and his smile widened.

"I thwarted Death too," I said, a few moments later. "Brodie cut my wrists and spilled my blood and if it hadn't been for Neely, I'd be nothing but a ghost. Does that mean Death is watching me too, waiting for another chance? Freddie used to say it wasn't right for me to think of death. She said it was unhealthy and grim and childhood was short and not to be squandered." I paused. "Still. If Death is coming for me I want to be prepared, Finch. Like you. I want to be brave and meet him halfway."

Finch grabbed my hand and held it tight. The bright sun sloped off his skin and he looked pale, but happy, his eyes bright, bright, bright. "You will, Vi. I promise."

I heard a groan from below deck. A River groan. He sounded like he was in pain, but I couldn't bring myself to care. I just kept standing next to Finch, and watching the sea.

≈≈≈

The mainland. We stood in the Nags Dune hardware store parking lot by Neely's car. River was so pale. He leaned against his brother, eyes closed. Two bruises were blossoming on his face, one from the driftwood and one from Neely's fist, and they made him look even more helpless. Which pissed me off. He wore some of Neely's clothes now, just like Finch, and they hung loose on his starved sea king body. Fragile blue veins snaked across his eyelids, and his breath was rasping and frail. He seemed made of nothing but seawater and air. He looked . . . drained. More than Finch even, who had died and come back to life only a handful of hours before.

River kept rubbing his eyes and sighing and if I still had a heart I probably would have felt sorry for him.

But I didn't.

He was supposed to stop and he broke his promise and now he was paying the price.

The color had gone out of my world, watching River push Finch underwater and hold him there until he drowned. The color went out, just like Freddie, and Will, and *rocking back and forth, back and forth, her hair swinging between his elbows, blood soaking them both.*

Canto put her back against the hood of the car and crossed her arms. Her black hair was un-brushed and curling up into tight ringlets in the morning mist. Her black eyes shifted, and looked River up and down. "So who is this?"

Neely moved River so he leaned against the car. River

couldn't have looked less scary, right then, less like a sea king who had glowed up an island and drowned a red-headed forest boy and maybe even a dark-eyed Finnfolk too.

Neely gave Canto a deep look, and then nodded at River. "This is my brother. He went missing and we found him, finally, on Carollie. He's sick with the flu, and he's a bit delirious with fever. Nothing to worry about, though."

Turned out Neely was a pretty good liar too.

I looked at River, and then at Canto. "Does he . . . does River look familiar to you, Canto?"

I felt Finch go still beside me.

Canto looked . . . lost . . . for a second, and then shook her head. "No. Why would he look familiar? Did he eat at the Hag's Shack sometimes?"

I shook my head, and then Finch did too.

Canto's lost look disappeared and her eyes went dark. "You're all hiding something from me."

"All in good time, Canto." Neely picked up Canto's blue suitcase, opened the trunk, and put it alongside his own expensive leather one.

"All in good time," Canto repeated. "Finch asks me to come with on a little trip, and he says it in such a way that I agree before I know what I'm doing. I leave my house, the Hag's Shack, my island, everything, and now I find out

I'm traveling with a sick person and a bunch of liars."

Neely laughed, and closed the trunk with a slam. "You're the one who jumped at Finch's invitation without even knowing where we were going. I can just picture you—dreaming of adventure every night while sweating over the grill at the Hag's Shack. Deny it. I dare you."

Canto rubbed the tip of her short nose with the palm of her hand. "Fair enough. I've been itching to escape this island for a few days. My father gets to run around and see the world"—she threw a hand out toward the water—"so why not his daughter too? Carollie has nothing to keep me. Not anymore."

"Isn't she a firecracker," Finch said, his eyes on Canto, nothing but Canto.

"Neely," I asked, because somehow no one had, "where are we going?"

Neely shrugged, and gave me one of his big grins.

I grinned back. I couldn't help it.

I looked up. The sky above was bright and blue and happy too, as if it didn't give a damn about whether Brodie was in Maine, or Colorado, or wherever the hell he was.

"I say we check out that town in the Rockies," Neely said, answering my question. "The one with the talking trees and the missing kids. *Tall, thin, red-haired girl.* That's good enough for me."

"Neely's got another sibling who might be in Colorado," Finch explained, eyes still on Canto.

Canto raised her eyebrows. "Another missing sibling? Neely, you know what they say—T*o lose one sibling may be regarded as a misfortune; to lose two looks like carelessness.*"

Neely laughed and laughed.

"Colorado is really far," I said. "Too far to follow a rumor that's probably just nothing. I'm worried about Luke and Sunshine and Jack and that damn barn boy."

"It's only three days, doing ten hours each," Neely said. "I'll drive fast."

I looked at River, gaunt and pale, still leaning against the car. He squeezed his eyelids shut against the sun and sighed softly. Then I looked at Neely.

I'd said yes to North Carolina without thinking.

Of course, we'd found River there, in the end.

"Call Luke from the road," Neely added. "Make sure everything up north is all right. If there's anything strange going on, anything at all, we'll turn around." He came up behind me and put his hands on my waist and his lips to my ear. "I don't want to bring River back to Citizen Kane, not while he's like this, Vi. I'm worried about your parents. And Jack. And Luke. And Sunshine. Let's give him a few days to recover, okay?"

"Okay." Neely was right. Taking a weak, disoriented,

sea king ex-boyfriend back to Maine to meet my parents seemed just about the stupidest thing I could do right then.

Neely laughed. Not a triumphant, I get my way laugh. Just his usual sweet, contagious laugh that brought me to my knees the same as River's damn crooked smile.

Neely, don't you take anything seriously?

He didn't. Mostly he didn't.

And I both hated this about him, and loved it.

I started smiling, hearing his laugh. I couldn't help myself, damn it.

"Good," Neely said, grinning at me. "Let's do this."

CHAPTER 17

ON THE ROAD. I sat in the backseat with River, because Canto said that if we put some delirious, flu-ridden stranger next to her, brother or no, she'd cut out his heart and throw it out the window. So she was up front with Neely, where I used to be, and I sat between River on one side, and Finch on the other.

We went west. The miles passed. The hours passed. River slouched against the side of the car. He still smelled like the sea. Salt and wind and death and life and sand.

And then the singing began.

"We'll kick up our forces like true wild horses. We'll rant and we'll roar across the salt deep. We'll worship the white and give up the fight, for here lies the wreck of the violet leap."

River had a fine voice, soft and low and true, and he sang

the words in sweet, lullaby tones. But the face the song came out of was hollow and bruised and wind-whipped and mad. I didn't recognize the River I used to know in it. Not anywhere.

River stopped singing, groaned, and started tugging at his sweater. "I can't wear these human clothes, Vi," he whispered to me. "They rub my fins wrong."

Neely laughed.

Finch looked at me, and raised his eyebrows in a way that didn't let me know what he was thinking at all.

But Canto glanced over her shoulder from the front seat, and watched River, and her expression was alert and wary. "Neely, your brother seems really sick."

Neely shifted his hands on the steering wheel and kept his eyes on the road. "He's fine. He's just got to burn the fever out."

Canto kept watching River. "He doesn't look fine."

"We're off the island and River is going to get better now," Neely answered in a sharp, non-Neely voice. "So let's stop talking about it."

Canto frowned, and turned back to the road.

River slumped against the door, sweater shoved to the side. He was half naked again, his lean chest clean and sea-salt free. He leaned toward me, and—

"My brother is keeping secrets," River whispered, quiet,

quiet, right in my ear. "I can tell. Neely always gets cranky when he lies."

River moved his lips away from my cheek again. I stared at him from the corner of my eyes, stared at the way his torso curved into the top of his black wool trousers . . .

I remembered. I remembered *breathing in, and feeling soft skin under my cheek and warm breath in my hair, in the shack, with the nets and the seaweed, and he slept like an angel, and his heart pumped against my palm, like waves hitting the shore, and I took off my seaweed dress and lay down on the nets, and River started stroking my arms, just his fingertips, all the way, top to bottom, and I . . .*

Finch put his hand on mine. I opened my eyes. He looked at me and shook his head. "Careful, Vi."

I shivered and moved closer to Finch's side of the car.

Finch noticed things. He noticed things Neely didn't.

River used to notice things. He used to notice everything.

But now he was just a sea king. A half-mad singing sea king.

Canto started grilling Neely from the front seat, despite what he'd said. "What if River gets worse on the way to Colorado? Fevers are deadly, Neely. Maybe we should find a hospital."

"He won't get worse," Neely said. "Violet's with him

now. She'll help him get well again. Tell them about the nightmares, Vi."

I sighed. "Last summer I slept next to River every night and he stopped getting his nightmares."

Neely winked at me in the rearview mirror. "See? River isn't going to get worse. Not when Violet's here. She makes him better."

I flinched.

Canto looked at me, full of doubt. Even Finch looked . . . wary.

Finch thinks Neely is lying, I thought. *And maybe he is.*

My heart was so disturbed it skipped a beat.

"He could have a concussion, Neely." I reached forward and put my hand on his shoulder.

Neely shook his head. "He doesn't. I checked. Volunteer EMT, remember? He's just tired and suffering the consequences of too much glow and too little food."

Canto stared at Neely. "Too much *glow*? What do you mean?"

No one answered her, and she frowned again. "Whatever it is, you're going to have to tell me eventually."

"You don't want to know," Finch whispered. "You don't." He leaned forward, moved Canto's hair, and kissed her cheek, slow and calm, just the once. Canto kept her eyes on the window, but she smiled. She did.

We stopped for a late lunch in the Appalachian Mountains. Neely pulled over at a scenic viewpoint. An ocean of trees stretched out all the way to the damn horizon. I didn't know there were so many trees in the whole world.

I wondered where Inn's End was, hidden in that forest. Maybe it had disappeared into the mist, like in the stories. I watched Finch, tried to catch his expression as he looked down. But his eyes were steady, no wildness anywhere, and no longing either.

There was snow on the ground again, and I was glad for it. I handed out apples from the picnic basket, and cheese, and the rest of the olives. River was still shirtless, and he'd kicked off Neely's extra pair of shoes too. He stood in the snow with his bare feet and refused to touch any of the food.

"I only eat seaweed and raw fish," he said, voice gentle. "Like all my kind."

"Well, we don't have either of those." Neely's voice was patient, but his eyes were a bit sad.

River ran his fingers through his long brown hair in a gesture that I remembered so well, so damn well, that it made me shudder a little bit. Then he waved his hand out in front of him. "The entire ocean floor is our dinner table. All we need to do is gather the bounty."

"We aren't on the ocean floor," Finch said, patient, just

like Neely, just like he'd been talking to mad sea kings his whole life.

Canto watched River. Closely. Her brow furrowed up and her dark eyes looked worried. Worried and . . . scared.

River is acting batshit crazy, Freddie. How can Canto believe this is just a fever? Is she starting to remember? What will we do if she does?

"Then what is all that blue above us?" River pointed at the sky. "It's the top of the ocean. See those white fluffy streaks? That's where the water has been stirred up from the fishing boats." He paused. "Isn't it?"

"That's the sky. That's just the damn sky, River." I looked at Neely. "How long is this going to last?"

"Not long," Neely answered, quick, sharp, his eyes refusing to meet mine. "The madness just has to run through him. It'll break soon."

My face felt hot, suddenly, blood churning and boiling, spreading down to my throat, arms, legs, feet.

Neely was lying.

"Safe in your bed you are at last." River was singing again, gentle, gentle, almost a whisper. *"Let the waters roar, Jack. All night long the storm did blast. Let the waters roar, Jack. Mind the shadows and watch your back. Let the waters roar, Jack. Riddle it out, find the shack. Let the waters roar, Jack."*

"You're all hiding something from me," Canto said

again, her voice drowning out River's singing. "And I hate it."

She threw her apple core into the snow and got back in the car.

Finch followed. And then River, still singing softly under his breath.

It was just me and Neely and the trees.

The sun broke through the clouds and hit the side of his face. I saw a darkening there that wasn't shadow.

"You have a bruise." I put my fingertips to his cheek. His face felt so much more familiar now. It felt more . . . mine. Whether I wanted it to or not. "Did this happen last night? Did River hit you too?"

But Neely just shook his head and got back in the car.

≈

We crossed the mountains and were camping in the snow again. The campground was closed, but we drove in anyway and set up our tents, no harm done.

I sat on a log and shivered and read Freddie's diary with a flashlight. Finch sat next to me. Canto built a fire with the driest wood she could find. I watched her for a while. Sometimes she seemed kind of . . . shy around Finch, and wouldn't look him in the eye.

Canto likes him, I realized. *She really likes him. He's making her self-conscious.*

After being on her own for so long . . . well, I understood. There was something about Finch sometimes that felt so . . . safe. Safe, snug, out of harm's way. Neely gave me that feeling, once in a while.

I looked at Cornelius Redding, sitting at the snow-covered picnic table cleaning the trout he bought from three fisherman we'd encountered earlier on the road. He looked up often, keeping an eye on his brother—who so far had done nothing but stand at the edge of the trees and stare into the snowy dark.

"No need to cook mine, Neely," River called over his shoulder. "I'll eat it just as it is."

Canto stared at River's back. "What are you going to do, rip it apart raw with your teeth? Neely, I'm really starting to worry about your brother."

Neely laughed, and it was dark, and harsh, and not at all familiar. "He's just eccentric. He's always been eccentric."

River turned around and caught my eye. And I saw it. The glint. The Redding glint was sparkling in his brown eyes again, and he wanted me to know. His breath froze as it hit the air—

"And the red red boy said good-bye to the seas and he took to the hills and he talked to the trees. 'Cause when the lone star sparks and the lone star shines, I'll look to my own, to the blood and the lines—"

"Eccentric or no," Canto snapped, "if he keeps singing I'll take that knife of yours, Neely, and cut him open when he sleeps."

Finch frowned, and Canto softened. "His singing is giving me the creeps, Finch. It reminds me of something. A bad dream I had once, I think."

Finch said nothing. He just put his hand on her arm and nodded.

River looked at me and smirked. It was fast—fast as a blink. But I saw it.

We sat on a long log before a roaring fire in a campground somewhere in Tennessee and ate hot fish with salt and lemon. I was between River and Finch, and my body finally started to warm up from the fire, at least the part of me that faced the flames.

My gaze drifted down, down to River's hands next to me, long fingers picking at his food.

Those hands had pushed Finch's face underwater until he died from it.

Finch, whose red hair was touching my blond on one side, and Canto's black on the other.

Snowflakes started falling. Big fat ones. I turned my palms over to face the sky, and the flakes fell on my skin and melted at my touch.

Neely started laughing at something Canto said. His

face in the firelight was tired. I wondered if anyone else had noticed how tired he looked all of a sudden.

We had kissed the night before, we had, it hadn't been a dream, River's brother, me, it was real. Neely had laughed and done it again and my stomach had melted right down to my toes, just as the snowflakes were melting on my fingertips.

River threw the rest of his fish into the fire and then looked right through me toward the trees. The glint was gone and his eyes were odd and dull and nothing else.

I glanced over at Neely, sitting on the other side of Canto, telling her one of his rich-boy stories, a grin shining under his tired eyes.

Finch reached out his hand and set it on my open palm, nestling his thumb up next to mine. And my anger started settling back down, right back down.

"Are you all right?" I asked him. We were all so focused on River that it was easy to forget Finch had died the night before. "Finch, are you sure you're all right? You still look too pale."

Finch nodded, once, as cool as ever. His red hair had started shining again. Or maybe it just looked that way in the firelight.

I slid my hand out of his and got to my feet. I readied the moka pot and set it near the fire, and in a few minutes it was rattling and steaming. River sniffed the air and seemed to perk up a bit. His eyes started sparkling again and his shoulders straightened.

"Is that espresso?" he asked. The glint was back, just like that, and the smile too, that damn crooked smile.

"Yes, River," I said.

"I haven't had coffee in a long, long time."

I poured the joe into one of the blue tin camping cups we'd brought along and then handed it to him. He took a sip, and then sighed.

"I smell like salt. And the sea." River took another sip. "Why the hell do I smell like the sea, Vi?"

"You used to be a sea king on a North Carolina island," I said. I poured myself a mug of coffee too, and drank. "You lived in a hut and slept on fishing nets and tried to drown a red-haired forest boy as a sacrifice. Do you remember?"

River didn't answer.

Later, Neely turned on the radio in the car and we listened to Wide-Eyed Theo. He talked about the same mountain town in Colorado again, the one we were heading to, but this time he focused on the rumor of "a Highlander hung up dead in a tree." At the very end, he mentioned that the town was still looking for the red-haired girl that stole the children.

A bad feeling started blossoming across my stomach. Queasy. Deep.

What if we finally find Brodie in Colorado, Freddie? Or another Redding half sibling, just as mad? What will we do?

The thought scared me so much I felt sick. So I stopped thinking about it.

I gave Finch the rest of my mug, and put the moka pot in the snow to cool so I could brew another round.

River drank the rest of his joe in one long swallow. He leaned toward me, smooth, his too-long hair falling across his forehead. His arms snapped out and wrapped around my waist. He pulled me into his lap.

My body folded into his like it had a mind of its own, my hip into the curve of his elbow, my face into his neck, my cold nose into the warmth of his bruised chin.

"Violet," he whispered into the top of my head, "would you sleep next to me tonight?" He kissed my temple, slow and soft, and I didn't stop him. "I keep having the nightmares. They won't leave me alone. Night after night." He put his hand on my wool-skirted knee, and then a little higher, his thumb moving in a small arc across my thigh. "Sometimes I dream that I'm using my glow on people and hurting them and I can't seem to stop. I just can't stop. Would you please sleep next to me, like old times?"

My eyes slid to Neely's. He was watching us. He met my gaze, blue to blue. He didn't smile. He didn't laugh. He didn't do anything. He just looked at me.

"Okay, River," I said.

The thing was, River needed me.

I think he needed me.

I could feel Finch's eyes, tickling the back of my neck as I slid off River's lap and went over to the coffeepot and the fire.

But he didn't say anything either.

I glanced again at Neely as I followed River into his tent, and he nodded and gave me one of his big Neely smiles.

But his eyes were dark and sharp and his hands twitched at his sides.

≈≈≈

River curled up in my arms in the cold just as I had curled up in his, all those nights last summer. And on the one hand it was not at all like I remembered. And on the other hand . . . it was.

I put my face in River's hair. He smelled like the sea. Not like leaves and autumn and midnight, but salt and wind and brine. Maybe he always would. He'd lived in that hut for God knew how long, his pores soaking in the ocean scents, his mind soaking in the glow. But the sea was a familiar smell to me, and so I guess I didn't mind. Maybe I even liked it.

There were no wolves howling this time, but the wind

was doing what it could, blowing through the trees like it was trying to impress somebody, shaking the walls of the tent, and making me shiver in River's arms.

"I screwed up, didn't I," River said, clear as a bell, long after I thought he'd fallen asleep.

"Yes," I whispered back. "Yes, River. You really, really screwed up."

And he held me, tight, his lean arms crisscrossing my back and his long brown hair sliding between my blond and it was just like before. I tried to see the wild horses in my head but I couldn't remember what they looked like and then River's hands moved under blankets and under clothes and my breath sped up and so did his and suddenly the cold wind couldn't touch me, I was that warm . . .

≈≈

River tossed and turned and cried out in his sleep.

Nightmares, nightmares.

I couldn't help River with his bad dreams this time. Not after what he'd done. Not after all that glow.

Chapter 18

March

Will writes and writes.

He says he needs me.

He begs.

And sometimes I can't say no. So I don't.

He comes back, and it's the two of us again, like old times, like always. I do whatever he asks, give him whatever he wants. I strip naked in the cemetery and hold him in the dark between the stones. I drink too much gin and lie across the train tracks tempting fate while he smiles at me and tells me I'll live forever. I lure nosy Shanna Shard to the sea and lead her into the waves, though she never did learn how to swim.

Those are the things I remember.

What about the things I don't?

I think Will is better. He always seems so much better.

I'm too happy. I miss the signs.

Lucas knows about Will and me. And he knows about the painter too. But he says nothing. Not a word.

I think God is punishing me.

≈≈≈

The next morning the sea king was back.

"I pushed him beneath the waves," River said. He wasn't singing this time, just talking softly. He stared out the window at the snowy scenes passing by, and seemed not to know where he was, or who I was, or anything at all. "I pushed him beneath the waves with little fuss, just like the sea king did before us."

I felt hate bubbling up inside me, strong as steaming black coffee.

Last night, you and me in the tent . . . none of it made any difference, River?

I moved a few inches over to Finch's side of the car.

He and Canto had shared a tent the night before and Canto had been quiet and soft-eyed over our hard-boiled-eggs-and-coffee-breakfast.

Finch's hair looked redder.

Every so often he would lean forward and touch Canto's curly black hair, softly, gently. Canto would laugh and the tip of her nose would turn pink.

Finch looked serious and calm and deep and happy.

I watched them, and kind of shivered with envy for a second, and River stared out the window, and Neely kept his eyes on the road.

If Neely was thinking about me, and River, and the both of us in the tent the night before . . . he hid it well. He looked slightly up to no good and overall pretty amused with life in general. As always.

Though he still looked tired. Really damn tired.

And suddenly I wanted it, all of it, every last bit of it, to disappear. Finch, Canto, River, the car, the road, gone, gone, gone.

I wanted to be back in the guesthouse, smelling snow in the air, Christmas Eve, Neely stretched out beside me, laughing, not looking tired, not at all.

I wanted it so much I *ached.*

"Just like the sea king did before us," River repeated, next to me.

I sighed.

"You're not a sea king," I said, though my eyes were on Finch now, on the way his calloused forest fingers touched

Canto's arm. "You're just a screwed-up rich boy with a glow."

"What's a *glow,* damn it?" Canto asked. And then frowned when no one answered.

River slid his hand onto my knee, and I turned to him, and I thought, *Here we go, he's going to remember, after last night, he's going to try to shake off his madness, he's—*

River opened his mouth—

"The flinchy bastard likes to tease, and you shall sink to the bottom of the seas. We poor sailors are skipping at the top while the citizens fall to their knees. The trees are talking and the lake will freeze, and all our brains will pop and squeeze . . ."

The River in the tent was not the River sitting next to me now. That River would have glowed up this River and made him slit his own throat.

When would this madness leave him? How much longer could we all take it?

"Stop singing," Canto shouted, her black hair flying as she flipped around, her curves pulling against the seat belt. "I can't stand listening to it. It makes me feel like screaming. Like crying, and screaming . . ." There were tears in Canto's eyes, and I wanted to tell her right then, tell her everything, because I knew what it felt like to be glowed up and not remember . . .

Except it would only make everything worse, so much worse. If Canto remembered Finch drowning, and River making him . . .

If she thought of the missing Finnfolk boy, and guessed what had happened to him . . .

No, I couldn't tell her. I couldn't.

But what if she remembers on her own, Freddie? What then?

Finch leaned forward and said calming, lullaby things to Canto.

River ignored all of us and kept whisper-singing.

Neely yanked on the wheel and pulled the car over to the side of the road. He turned around in his seat and stared at his brother. Hard. "Enough with the singing, River. I mean it."

River's voice trailed off. And, after a couple of heartbeats, his eyes cleared, and his posture . . . changed. He stopped sitting straight-backed like a king, hands on his knees. He relaxed into the back of the seat, and his arms and legs went long and lazy, like the old River.

Neely turned back around and then we were driving again, the car silent.

After that, River didn't sing or chant strange sea things or try to take his sweater off or announce that he only ate raw fish and seaweed. Not once.

Except. Except for the time he leaned toward me and whispered in my ear, *"Violet, who are these people?"*

And he was looking at Neely when he said it.

≈

I'd tried to call the Citizen from a pay phone three times since we left Carollie. But no one answered the first two times and the third time the line had been disconnected.

If I wasn't around, no one remembered to pay the phone bill.

I hoped that was the problem, anyway.

Please let that be why, Freddie.

We stopped at a general store in a quiet, sweet town named Spring Green. I called Sunshine's house from the pay phone. No one answered. I left a message on the machine, saying we were headed to Colorado.

We couldn't find a campground, come dusk that night. There was nothing but emptiness and snow and small bunches of strange bent trees that looked as if they were huddling together in the cold. Finally Finch spotted the roof of a building—it was down a neglected side road that was almost hidden by tall pines. We turned in, and drove slowly forward, hoping, hoping, hoping it would be abandoned.

"Well, it's no Lashley house," Neely said as we all climbed out of the car.

And it wasn't. It was in bad shape. Peeling white paint and half the roof collapsed and boards missing from the front steps. The few, unbroken windows were thick with dirt and covered with tattered curtains.

This big farmhouse had a family in it once, Freddie. And rosebushes that blossomed every summer and scruffy dogs running around and lazy firefly nights and evening thunderstorms that shook its walls and made the kids shiver in their beds. What the hell happened between then and now?

I always wondered that, about abandoned houses.

Neely went up and tried the door. It was locked, or jammed. He shook it a few times, hoping to dislodge it. The house creaked, and then something big and heavy on the other side of the door hit the ground. The thud was so deep I felt it in my chest, like a heartbeat.

"You're going to shake the house down," River said in his old River voice, clear and sly. "And then where will we sleep?"

Neely laughed, and shrugged.

We walked around to the back of the house, and found the family cemetery. Just fourteen gravestones worn to nothing, peeking their heads out of the snow as if too shy to show themselves. We put up our tents between the stones, since it was the only clearing wide enough. Mother Nature was taking the land back and trees hugged the house from all sides.

"I seem to be spending a lot of my life in cemeteries lately," I said, to no one in particular. "But I think it suits me."

Luke would have yelled at me for saying that. He would have told me to stop being so stupid and odd.

I missed him, suddenly.

I was worried about my brother. About the whole Citizen crew. Jack and Sunshine and my parents. I worried about them all the damn time, every damn second I wasn't worried about Neely. Or River.

Finch set up my tent in front of two small gravestones that leaned together, as if they were whispering in each other's ears.

We'd bought dry firewood and coal and food at the general store and had a supper of red potatoes wrapped in foil with butter and carrots and onions and black pepper and lemon juice and sea salt. Canto called it Hobo Potatoes and cooked it on the rocks near the flames and it was just about the best thing I'd ever tasted. There was an icy-cold stream that ran through the property, and we drank it straight and freezing cold, and then got some more to use for coffee.

River was quiet. He hadn't sung since Neely told him to shut up. We all huddled up to the fire, wincing each time the wind blew through the broken-roofed house and made it groan and sigh.

Finch sat near Canto by the flames. I might have shivered again, watching them. Or maybe it was just the cold. Finch and Canto. The Feisty Island Maid and the Forest Boy. It would make a good story, told by a fire.

My own story had morphed from the Mysterious Liar and the Lonely Granddaughter into the Mad Sea King and the Red-Haired Orphan Rescuer Who Made Bad Choices.

Which was the better story?

Which was the *true* story?

Finch would know. I had a feeling Finch would know . . . not that I could go ask him. Canto's cheek was pressed up against his shoulder and they were talking quietly to each other.

I shivered again.

"I'm so glad you didn't drown," I said out loud to Finch, before I knew what I was doing.

Neely gave me a kind of wide-eyed look but Finch just nodded. "Thank you, Violet," he said. And then he got up and filled River's blue cup with espresso from the moka pot.

River, the boy who had shoved Finch's head underwater until it killed him.

"When did you almost drown, Finch?" Canto asked. "Was it when you were a child? You should tell me that story."

"I will," Finch answered, not meeting her eyes. "Someday."

"Hey . . . are you Brodie?" River asked. He was staring at Finch's red hair in the red firelight, the way it shone like a damn red star. "Are you the boy with the knife?"

We all froze.

The fire crackled and the wind howled and none of us moved an inch.

River nodded, still staring at Finch. "If so, then . . . I was right to drown you."

Finch and River stared at each other, stared and stared.

"It's not him," I said. "This is Finch, a boy we met in the Appalachian Mountains."

River gave Finch one more long look. And then he just shrugged and held out his mug for more coffee.

Canto's round face suddenly looked almost . . . *mean.* "Neely, I don't think your brother is sick or eccentric. I think he's fucking with us."

Neely laughed. "Could be, Canto. Could be."

Canto didn't laugh with him. She opened her mouth—

"Let it go," Neely said, and he wasn't laughing now. Not at all. *"Let it go."*

She did.

A raven cawed. I looked up and saw him on the roof of the house, black outline against the black night sky, waiting for us to disappear so he could have at the scraps of our supper.

One of the bigger logs collapsed, and the fire roared up another two feet.

And I saw it. Neely had another bruise on his face, left cheek now, near his jaw.

There's something to those bruises. I wonder if he knows . . .

And the more I thought about it, the more I realized that yep, he probably did.

My wrists started tingling then, a sharp ache that wasn't helped by the cold.

Two Redding brothers, both with bruises.

It all felt so familiar, suddenly. Round and round and played out and started back up again.

Finch had seen the new bruise too. He stared at Neely as the firelight glinted off his face, and Finch's expression grew . . . worried. And Finch never looked worried. Not even right before River made him drink the sea. Not even then.

≈≈

There were no crisscrossing arms and hands under blankets and breath speeding up in the tent that night. River just curled into me and went right into deep sleep, his skin smelling less like salt than the night before, less like sea and more like cold boy.

I lay there for a few minutes, thinking about how un-mad River probably wouldn't want me kissing sea-mad, sea king River. He would probably see it as . . . unfaithful.

The problem was, I never knew which River I was going to get anymore.

I wondered what River would think about me kissing his own damn brother.

River would glow Neely up and screw the consequences and call it justified while he was at it.

I was Freddie's granddaughter, after all. I couldn't kiss one person without it pissing another person off.

My feet crunched in frozen snow as I stepped around the small gravestones.

"Canto?" Neely called into the dark as I unzipped the little door.

And that cut me a little bit. It did. Right in the softest part of my heart.

But then I heard a quiet little laugh, and the sound of a match skidding. A fat white candle began to glow with light. Neely was sitting up, looking at me.

"Hey you," he said, and grinned.

"Take it off," I said. "Your shirt. Take it off."

When he didn't move, I said it again. "Take off your shirt. There's something I want to see."

The Redding glint disappeared from his eyes, along with his smile, snap, gone, just like before, when Canto was talking about River fucking with us.

He looked older, without that damn careless smile on

his face, without the damn sparkle in his eyes. He looked like . . . a fighter. Like he could beat the hell out of someone and enjoy doing it.

"Take your shirt off," I said, again.

"You're getting as bossy as that Carollie girl." Neely set the candle down and began tugging up his finely knit, rich-boy sweater.

I looked at Neely, at the long scar that ran from his neck to his right wrist—a scar that River gave him, though he hadn't meant to. But it wasn't the scar I'd come to see. Black and blue and purple, four of them stretching across his torso, each the size of my fist.

"Neely." I put my hands on his chest. I ran my fingertips over his ribs. "You're covered in bruises."

"Yes."

"And you haven't been fighting."

"No."

"Tell me what's going on."

"You already know what's going on."

Neely shuddered as my fingers moved across his skin, but whether it was from pain, or something else, I didn't know.

"You have a glow," I said, because suddenly I knew, I just knew. *"You've had a glow all along."*

Neely paused.

Shook his head.

Nodded.

"I have a . . . it's more like an anti-glow. It's not the same thing. It's . . . it's why I'm not worried about River. I've temporarily castrated him, so to speak. He couldn't use his glow now if he tried."

"How long have you known?" I asked. My hand touched his arm, my fingers going up and down the fire-scar.

"I've suspected for a while. I started putting two and two together last summer, after everything that happened in Echo. But I wasn't sure until we got River away from Carollie, and I tried again. I didn't know this kind of Redding glow was even possible. Which is why it took so long for me to figure it out. Things make a lot more sense now. Like why River always got worse when he left home and I wasn't around. And the bruises . . . I was in so many fights I never knew the difference."

A few minutes passed, where we both just sat next to each other and thought.

"If you're anti-glowing River," I said, finally, "why is he still being the sea king?"

Neely shrugged. "I don't know. Maybe he used too much glow and went crazy with it, like Brodie. It'll pass. I know it will. He just needs time."

I kept moving my fingers on his scar and not meeting

his eyes. "You've got to stop, Neely. You can't keep this up." And, as if proving my point, he flinched when my fingers moved down and touched his ribs again.

He took short, fast breaths until I moved my hand. "I can't stop. I have to hold River in, keep him on a short leash." Neely breathed in. And out. Slower. Like it hurt. "At least until he stops being so damn crazy. When he's like this he's capable of anything."

"But what if he never quits being the sea king? What then?"

Neely shook his head. "He will, Vi. He'll come back to us. He just needs a break from the glow."

Maybe Neely was right. River had said something, right before he left last summer . . . something about his grandfather telling him he needed to abstain to get his control back. That's what he'd set off to do when he left. River was supposed to cut himself off so he could recover from too much glowing and stop losing control.

Of course, he broke that promise, in the end.

"What does it feel like?" I put the palm of my hand on another of Neely's bruises, and it felt hot. Even in the cold tent, it heated my hand right up. "Does it feel good, like the glow?"

Neely let out a small sigh. "No. Not at all. It feels like . . . a headache, mixed up with the smell of dust . . . and the color of rain, and . . . and a feeling of frustration."

"Neely," I said, not looking at him, only looking at my fingers. They wanted to move over his skin again, to make him shudder again. "If you keep doing this, keep getting the bruises and un-glowing River . . . what will happen?"

Neely laughed. "Who knows?"

"Will you go mad too?"

"I hope not, Vi. Then you'd have two singing sea kings on your hands."

I didn't laugh with him. "I'm scared. I'm scared for you." And my eyes snapped to his, and then back to the bruises, to the ones that spilled across his ribs from front to back, to the ones that made it hard for Neely to breathe.

It didn't seem fair that River's glow felt warm and good and made him a sea king when Neely's did . . . this.

"I'll be all right," Neely whispered. He paused. Put his hands on my hips. Brought me closer. "Violet?"

"Yes?"

"You . . . you should go back to bed. Back to River. He needs you."

He leaned into me then, close, close, and his lips brushed past mine, soft, soft, soft, and I could picture the wild horses again, picture their tails, and their warm breath fogging in the cold sea air, and the sand flying, and all of it, all of it.

“I don’t regret what I did,” Neely said, so low it was almost a whisper. He didn’t explain and I didn’t need him to. “Not for a second. No matter what happened afterward. No matter what’s going to happen now.”

“Neither do I.” And I didn’t realize how true it was until it came out of my mouth.

Neely kept his hands on me, and blew out the candle. His thumbs started moving in little circles over my hip bones. We both sat there in the dark and I was shaking a bit and I guess I knew why. My blood was pulsing and roaring like a damn baritone singing out some heartbroken aria on the stage.

But I didn’t move and I didn’t talk. I didn’t even sigh.

Neely said I was that kind of girl. Quiet on the outside and loud on the inside.

≈≈

Later, much later, I slipped out of the tent and back into the night. The nearby house kept up its creaking and sighing in the winter wind and it was creepy and beautiful at the same time. River opened his eyes when I slid in next to him, just for a second, and smiled at me before falling back to sleep. I held him in my arms and listened to his soft breathing—after a while it seemed to join up with the howling wind outside, as if they were singing in harmony.

I thought about life and death and sane and insane

and I was stirred up and wide-awake. Eventually my thoughts drifted to the people buried beneath me under the dirt and snow. Was one of them a girl my age? When did she die? Why? Maybe we were the same height. Maybe she was stretched out just like me, six feet down, and we were aligned head to head and toe to toe.

That thought comforted me, for some reason, and I finally fell asleep.

CHAPTER 19

RIVER WAS BETTER. He didn't scream in his sleep, not once. In the morning he rose before me and started the fire and brewed coffee in the moka pot. And when he poured espresso for the rumpled Canto and the quiet-as-ever Finch, they took it and acted like it was the most ordinary thing in the world.

"It looks like his fever broke, just like you said it would, Neely." Canto sat on the edge of the biggest gravestone, and Finch stood next to her, drinking his coffee.

Does Canto really believe that, Freddie?

Neely gave Canto a tired smile, and nodded. "I'm always right. Just ask Vi."

And then he looked at me, those damn blue eyes straight on mine, and that was all it took.

Neely, half naked, candlelight, ribs, bruises, the old house creaking, the tent walls flapping, Neely's thumbs on my hip bones, and I wanted it, I did, Freddie help me, I did . . .

River got in the front seat of the car when we were ready to leave, but no one said anything. It meant that I had to sit next to, and witness, the caresses of Canto and Finch. But hey, River's eyes were calm and he looked less starved and lost and almost...civilized. I didn't see the glint I loved or his crooked smile. But I wasn't complaining.

"You need a haircut," I yelled up to him at one point, somewhere in Kansas.

He turned back to me, eyes calm, face calm. "True. That's so damn true, Vi."

And it was the only thing he said all day, but it was enough.

River was doing better, way better.

But Neely . . .

Three times I saw him stop what he was doing and suck air in through his teeth. Neely was faded. Tired and faded. His bruises were even worse in the daylight. He was moving slower than usual. He couldn't keep up this thing, not for much longer.

Maybe we really would find Brodie in Colorado. And maybe that would change everything, somehow. Maybe we would find Brodie, and slit his throat, and then we could go back to Citizen Kane and let River be as crazy as he needed to be, and just wait him out, and Neely could stop.

Though if we were really getting closer to Brodie, wouldn't I feel it? Wouldn't I feel his nearness, deep in my bones?

Did I even want to find him?

I would be meeting Death halfway, at least. Like Finch. Staring my fear in the face. There was something likable, something . . . serene . . . in that. There was.

≈≈≈

The first part of Colorado was flat and straight and pretty in a wide-sky way. It was dark by the time we reached the mountains, though we could see the setting sun glinting off the snowy Rockies miles before we got anywhere near the foothills.

We were in the West. The place of cowboys and horses and cattle and gunfights and poker and saloons and riding off into the sunset.

Gold Hollow proved much easier to find than Inn's End. We stopped to buy a local map at a small Wild West store in a Colorado town named Esther Park. The crinkly-eyed man at the counter told us Gold Hollow was pretty much a ghost town compared to what it was in the gold rush days, but some stubborn mountain types still lived and raised their families there. And then he pointed to it right on the map.

So things were looking up, in that sense.

We wound our way up the mountain, up and up. Switchbacks and more switchbacks and ice and snow and slick and skid and no side-rails and thank God Neely's car could take it.

Neely's hands clung to the steering wheel and his shoulders hunched up tight to his ears. His eyes, when I saw them in the rearview mirror, looked so dull and worn out I kind of felt like screaming.

Finally, finally, the road curved down into a valley.

Gold Hollow stretched out in a small dip of land, ending in a lake and surrounded by snowy peaks, the stars and the sky wide open above it all. It was a mix of abandoned miners' shacks and solid, well-maintained log cabin homes. There was one small little white church up the hill at the end of the street. Cool rusted-out cars from the fifties and sixties sat amid tree stumps and scattered log huts in the snow-filled meadow that broke up the middle of the town. Being the vintage-loving boy that he was, River smiled when he saw the cars, and it made me smile too. It did.

The town was dark. Quiet. I saw a few lights on, but no one was out and about. Which might not have had as much to do with Inn's End–ishness as it did the fact that it was dark, and winter, and suppertime, and the town looked like there wasn't much to do in it anyway. I saw a weathered hotel, a general store, and a small, rickety café. And that was it.

Brodie could be here, I thought. *He could be standing up on that hill, or behind that tree, watching us right now, trying to decide which of us he's going to spark up first.*

But he wasn't.

I had a feeling, suddenly. A deep-in-the-gut feeling. It had been building for the past two days and suddenly something about the white church and the meadow and the rusted cars broke it out of me.

Brodie wasn't in Colorado.

He was in Riddle.

I hadn't been able to reach Luke and Jack or anyone and I knew why.

Brodie had disconnected the phone and was sparking them all up and it was too late and I shouldn't have gone to North Carolina, I followed Neely, why had I done that? *It was so stupid, so very stupid, Freddie, I—*

I shook myself, hard.

One step at a time. Just figure out where you're staying the night first. You can't make Neely drive all the way back to Maine right now anyway. And you don't know that Brodie's there. You don't know that at all. So shut your mouth and keep it together.

We parked the car outside the hotel, which, despite all expectations, appeared open. It was a big, boxy, wooden two-story building, white, with three rows of square windows, a long wraparound porch, and white letters on the top that said *Hollow Miner Hotel.* Definitely a step up from sleeping on the ground.

"How much money do we have left?" Neely asked.

"Not much." I looked at River. If he'd had money before he went to Carollie it was long, long, long gone.

"I can pay my own way," Canto said. And that decided it.

The front door was heavy, and creaked when I pushed it open. We stepped into a large room. Red rugs covered a hardwood floor, and hand-carved wooden furniture filled up the corners. An oversized fireplace was stoked and flaming and spitting out heat. The whole thing was so Wild, Wild West, it warmed the damn cockles of my heart.

There was a bar off to the side, and the large mirrors that lined the wall reflected shiny bottles of booze. A bright-eyed woman with narrow shoulders stood behind the counter. Her smooth white hair was cut in a neat bob and she looked like such an exact combination of Freddie and Agatha Christie's Miss Marple that I was drawn to her like flies to honey.

"Are you looking for a place to stay?" she asked, waving her small fingers in the air in hello.

We walked toward the counter, and set our suitcases down. "Well, how much is it for a room?" I asked.

She blinked clever Miss Marple eyes. "Forty dollars for a double bed with the bathroom down the hall and meals included. We're usually filled up with skiers this time of year, but the road into Gold Hollow has been in such bad shape the last few days that the snowheads had to go elsewhere. How did you five make it here?"

"Luck," Neely said, and half laughed. And then put a hand to his ribs.

Finch looked worried and I guess I did too.

Miss Marple eyed up the two bruises on Neely's face. "I hope you gave the mountain as good as you got. You snowheads. You think you're immortal."

She shook her head. And then, I swear, she actually clucked her tongue.

Neely didn't bother to correct her, because what would he say anyway? That he hadn't been skiing but instead had a strange power that stopped his brother's strange power, and it ran in their family, his brother's strange power, not his, his was the first of its kind, and . . .

. . . and that was already sounding so stupid in my head that I flinched.

Besides, Miss Marple was doing something interesting. Her small body was spinning and her fingers were dancing over the glistening bottles and the next thing Neely knew he had a shot of cognac sitting in front of him.

"Drink it," she said. "It will help."

Neely smiled. He tossed his head back and the lovely amber liquid disappeared. Miss Marple had already moved on down to Finch and River. "You two don't look quite right either. Here. Both of you."

And two more shots of cognac appeared, and then disappeared, down the throats of Finch and River.

I wondered if the local police knew there was a white-haired Agatha Christie character giving expensive shots of liquor to underaged kids down at the hotel. And then I realized that everyone probably knew, and didn't really care. Which was kind of beautiful, when you thought about it. I was starting to see the appeal of the West.

I reached down into my zippered skirt pocket and took out all the money I could find. I had no more origami animals, just odd bits of change.

"We'll take three rooms," I said. Which would leave us a little for gas and food and coffee and another night, if we needed it.

"By the way," Neely said, rubbing his right face-bruise with his hand. The cognac had made his cheeks go a bit pink. "You haven't heard anything about the trees around here. About them . . . talking . . . have you? Or about some kids that have gone missing? Or a tall, redheaded kid causing trouble?"

Miss Marple had started to ring us up on an old cash register. She paused, her small wrinkled fingers still on the buttons. "You must have been chatting with Wild Ann Boe. Our town gossip goes right off her rocker every year when the snow comes. After the first big winter storm, they found the Scotsman hanging naked, feet up, from a tree outside that isolated cabin of his. Such a big man as that, with that fiery orange hair. He hunted grizzlies, in his time. But someone had it in for him. You children are in the wilds, in case you don't know. There's not much difference between now and a hundred years ago, except the loss of the gold and the people that followed it."

She pushed a chunk of soft white hair behind her ear, and looked straight at me. "The snow set Wild Ann off, and the dead Scotsman just encouraged her. She started seeing all kinds of oddities again, just like last year, and all the years before. Omens in the sky. Portents in the rivers. And then the trees started talking to her, telling her to do things. Or so she said. If you ask me, Wild Ann is looking for attention more than sanity."

"So no children are missing?" Neely took a deep breath, and then put his hand to his ribs again. "There's no red-haired girl? No talking trees? There must be more to this story than just one gossip. We heard about it all the way on the East Coast."

Miss Marple shook her head. "It will trace back to poor Wild Ann, I'm afraid."

I knew it.

What now, Freddie?

"Neely," I said, not looking at him, keeping my eyes on Miss Marple. "Neely, we have to leave for Maine. *Tonight.*"

Miss Marple clucked her tongue again. "Haven't you heard? A storm is rolling in. Twelve inches of snow, plus wind. It's going to hit in a few hours. You're not going anywhere."

≈≈≈

The keys to our rooms were big and black, with the room number hanging from a metal tag on the end. They felt heavy in my hand, and solid, like they had a purpose and were proud of it.

The hallway of the second floor was narrow and dark and the floorboards creaked. Canto and Finch took the first room, Neely the second, River and me the third.

There was something so much . . . more, to sharing a hotel room with River instead of a tent. But he just followed me down the hall, and we didn't have enough money for another room anyway.

And if Neely looked at me over his shoulder in the hallway and if I looked at him over mine, well, what difference did it make.

None.

I set my suitcase on the bed and looked around. There was an old white sink in the corner. The bed was narrow for two people, but firm. The pink-striped wallpaper was turning brown with age, but otherwise the room was clean and airy enough.

Freddie, you have to watch out for Luke and Jack. And my parents. And Sunshine. You have to keep them safe. Freddie, are you listening?

"I do believe," River said, leaning one arm on the heavy wooden dresser, "that this place used to be a brothel, back in Gold Hollow's heyday."

I jerked myself out of my grim Brodie thoughts. River was talking. And it was clear and sane and made no reference to the sea. I needed to pay attention. "I suppose that's why it was only forty bucks, then."

River crooked-smiled at me, and his eyes were mischief and spark and sly. "Come over here, Vi. I want to see what it feels like to have you next to me with a warm roof over our heads."

I went over and stood next to him by the dresser. He hooked one finger through the belt loops on my wool skirt and pulled me closer.

"River," I said, kind of quiet, lifting my face to his. "River, I'm afraid Brodie is in Maine right now and hurting my brother and Jack. Where . . . where do you think he is?"

River shook his head, and his shaggy brown hair swept past my cheek. "No, Vi. He's not in Maine."

"How can you be sure?"

River just shrugged, and pulled out his old crooked smile again and shined it down on me.

God, it was good to have him back.

And then I remembered.

Neely, shirt off, body covered in bruises.

I squirmed out of River's arms and went over to the window. I opened it a crack, and breathed in. Miss Marple was right. A storm was coming. I could smell it on the air, cold and sharp and angry.

We gathered on the main floor of the hotel for supper. Miss Marple was also the cook, as it turned out. The five of us sat at a solid table on an elegant, worn rug next to a roaring fire. We ate creamy corn chowder from steaming white bowls and buttered brown bread and homemade hot chocolate spiked with rum.

And if it occurred to us as we ate that we drove halfway across the country based on the attention-starved ramblings of a town gossip, well, we just tucked into our meal and didn't say anything about it.

≈≈≈

The mountain storm began to blow just as River and I pulled back the covers and slid into bed. It rattled the windowpanes and howled at the doors and clawed at the cracks.

I dreamed River was kissing the hollow of my throat in the middle of a blizzard.

And when I woke up, he was.

He was warm as summer rain. Smooth as the sea, and twice as deep.

"Where did you get this necklace?" River asked. He moved the jade beads out of the way so he could reach the skin underneath.

Neely.

"Your brother," I answered, quiet, barely even whispering.

"Of course," River said. "It was our mother's. Our father gave it to her after our grandfather gave it to him. Did you know that?"

I shook my head.

"He must have gotten it out of the safety-deposit box in Switzerland, the bastard. You know, I was going to give this necklace to you for Christmas."

"River, what's my name?" I whispered into River's ear, just to check, just to be sure.

"Violet," he whispered back.

"And where are we?"

"In an ex-brothel called the Hollow Miner's Hotel. Gold Hollow, Colorado."

"And who are you?"

"The sea king, of course."

And then River's eyes were on mine and they were so bright and full of familiar rascality that I felt like laughing, and did.

"I'm back," River whispered. His arms went around me and he squeezed me up and he smelled like coffee and midnight again and not the sea, not the sea, not the sea. "I missed you, Violet. I missed you so damn much."

"What do you remember?" I asked, my body tight to his and his hands on my hips and my face against his shoulder.

"Bits and pieces. Enough." He paused. "Violet, can you ever forgive me?"

I didn't think about it, not even for a second. "No," I whispered. "I'll never forgive you."

But then we were kissing again, and oh, I was so happy,

I couldn't help it, sunshine was streaming out my fingertips and each and every atom in me was shaken up and sparkling with joy and I wanted everything to be like last summer, I wanted it so badly, and I knew this time it wasn't the glow making me feel this way, it couldn't be, Neely was making sure of that, Neely, what about Neely, no, don't think about it Violet, just enjoy this moment because it's not going to—

Footsteps in the hallway. The slap, slap of bare feet on bare wood. The creak of the floorboards and the doorknob turning because I'd forgotten to lock it because I wasn't used to locking things.

"Don't worry, it's not Brodie," River whispered.

The door opened.

He was right.

Canto flew across the room and had a knife at River's throat before I took my next breath. She leaned over the bed and her black curls fell on my bare upper back and it was warm and soft and terrifying. I tried to sit up, and the bed jolted.

The knife went in deeper. I saw blood.

"Canto, what are you doing?" And my voice sounded shrill to my ears and I hated it.

Finch slid out of the shadows in the hall. "She remembered," he said, his eyes on mine.

"Is it true?" Canto asked, ignoring me, ignoring Finch, her eyes on River, only River. *"Did you drown him?"*

Finch came forward and put his hand on Canto's right arm. "Why don't you hear him out before you gut him?"

Canto paused . . . and then pulled back the knife from River's throat. She moved to the end of the bed and just stared at us, her whole body shaking in little bursts.

"I told her that River went mad from the glow on Carollie, and that he drowned me," Finch whispered. "But I also told her that Brodie is the real villain. The one we hoped to find, out here in Gold Hollow. The one I was mistaken for in Inn's End."

Canto kept her hand on the knife and kept staring. River sat up. He put his fingertips to his throat and they came back wet and red.

Canto got up and stood with her back to the rattling window. "Let me tell you about Roman," she said.

And I squeezed my eyes shut at that, and pictured the boys at the Hag's Shack that first night, and the ones who held me and Neely and Finch on the beach, all of them beautiful and dark-eyed and looking just like the boy on the poster, and I was already sick with sadness before Canto even opened her mouth.

She had stopped shaking. Her arms were stiff at her sides now, her black hair in tight, tight curls. "Roman was a Finnfolk boy. He . . . we used to . . . He was special, even for a Finnfolk. And then one day he just disappeared. Everyone told me it was the Finnfolk way, that he'd gotten bored and run off to the mainland, like half his brothers before him. There was another girl, I knew about her all along, so I believed them . . ."

Canto walked back to the bed. She put her left hand on River's chest, and with her right she put the knife back to his throat. "You drowned him. Didn't you, River."

River didn't move. None of us did.

"You turned my whole island into your worshiping sea slaves every night just for the fun of it and you drowned Roman and then Finch and all of you lied to me about it when I didn't remember."

The knife went in, just a little, and blood began to drip again, drip down River's neck and chest and pool in the swoop of Canto's left hand where her thumb met her fingers.

"Canto, put the knife away," Finch said softly, red, red hair swinging as he shook his head. "Making River bleed won't bring Roman Finnfolk back from the dead."

Canto kept staring at River. She stared at him like he was a monster.

Or a god.

I'd looked at him like that too, once upon a time.

Then Canto reached her arm back and let out a howl. The knife went flying into the wall across the room, and stuck there. *"You killed him,"* she screamed.

And I didn't know which boy she was referring to, Roman or Finch. Both, I guess.

"Finch told me about Neely's bruises," she whispered, eyes on River's, still, still, all the steam gone out of her voice. "He figured it out. He figured out how Neely is the only reason you aren't glowing us all up right now and making us be your sea slaves, like before." She swiped her hands across her cheeks, quick, and then put them back down at her sides. "Do you . . . do you know what that did to me? Watching Finch drown and being too glowed up to do anything about it? And then made to forget for days afterward? You drowned a forest boy and the only person I've ever loved and yet no one here seems to care. Why doesn't anyone care?"

"I care." River. He'd said nothing up until now. Not one word. And then again. "Canto, I care."

Silence.

"I was trying to stop." River put his hands in his dark hair and made it even messier than it was from sleeping and kissing and almost having his throat slit. Blood oozed from the small cuts in his neck and slipped farther down his naked torso. "And I would have succeeded. I was holed up in Canada and not using the glow and everything was going well. I was hanging out on the docks and doing odd jobs when I heard about a story from a passing fisherman. He said there was a sea king with flaming red hair on a North Carolina island . . ." He paused, and I stared at him and his eyes looked deep and lost and sad, sad, sad. "I've started to remember. Bits and pieces. I remember getting to Carollie and . . . and Brodie was there and then he wasn't and then I was the sea king. I didn't drown Roman, Canto. But I think Brodie did."

Canto and Finch went stock-still, and me too, all of us just stunned and quiet.

Brodie? Brodie had been there first? Had drowned the Finnfolk boy, had sparked up River before going to Inn's End? It was Brodie, all along?

Canto screamed again. Tilted her head back and screamed. And then she was quiet again. The whole room was quiet again.

"It's the truth," River said. Finally. He blinked fast and his eyelashes grew shiny and wet. "For once, it's the truth."

Canto glared at River and seethed and seethed like she was the only person in the world who had a right to hate him.

And then, after a few long, long minutes, she started to cry.

Finch put his arms around Canto and led her out of the room, closing the door behind him.

River crawled back into my arms, and he didn't seem rascally or sly anymore. He just seemed . . . naked, and wide-open, and scared.

"It's going to be all right," I said. My hands pressed into his skin, trying to stop his shaking. "It's going to be all right," I said, again and again, though I didn't think it would. Not a bit. Not at all.

CHAPTER 20

I WOKE UP alone.

Neely and I found River talking to Wild Ann Boe outside in front of the hotel.

She had on a worn, green wool coat, and black boots. She had smooth brown hair and shifty gray eyes, though her smile was nice enough. She jerked when we opened the front door, and then darted across the porch right toward us.

"Have you heard?" she asked. "Have you heard about the missing children?"

I shook my head, but Neely nodded, and it seemed to encourage her.

"I saw them. I saw them following a tall young girl into the woods. She had red hair and played a tin whistle and wore a striped suit, just like in the *Pied Piper of*

Hamelin. She led them off into the darkness beyond the mountains."

The woman paused. Swallowed. Her hands were slim and red and shaking, and she seemed so upset, so genuinely upset, that I pitied her. I did.

"This happened before," she said. "The children up and disappearing all at once. Sixty years ago all the children followed a beautiful, brown-haired man into the mountains too, and never came back. And then the bear-killer Nathaniel Mellingsather was found cut to pieces next to his own shotgun. Now it's all happening again. Why doesn't anyone care? Why isn't anything being done?"

"Wild Ann Boe, don't you have somewhere to be?" Miss Marple appeared in the doorway behind us, wearing an apron and a cunning look on her small, pointed face.

Wild Ann stared at her. "The children," she repeated.

"Like those right there?" Miss Marple pointed to two eight- or nine-year-olds as they walked out of the café, their parents following behind.

Wild Ann opened her mouth. Closed it. Opened it again. "Edith, you have the Devil sleeping in your hotel. Did you know?"

Miss Marple sighed and shooed Gold Hollow's gossip away with a flick. Wild Ann turned and slunk off toward the general store.

"She's harmless. Mostly." Miss Marple, whose real name was Edith, gave us a shrewd-ish smile. "How did you two sleep last night? I thought I heard some screaming at one point, but that could have been the wolves. They get a little close in winter when the food is scarce."

She stared at us.

Neely didn't say anything. I didn't say anything. The ex-brothel walls were just about as thin as you'd expect them to be, I guess.

"So was it just the wolves, then?" Miss Marple asked.

I nodded, and then, a second later, Neely joined in. I swear I saw a twinkle, a damn twinkling twinkle, in Miss Marple's eyes. I guess she was used to mysterious screams in the night.

"It doesn't look like it now, but another storm is on its way." Miss Marple pointed one finger at the sky and one at Neely. "You're not going anywhere. Not today."

I whipped my gaze toward the peaks. She was right. I saw the line of dark, hovering.

Damn it.

A storm was coming, and there was a barn boy in Maine, and no Brodie in Colorado, and Neely was looking more pale and tired every damn minute, and now we were stuck here again, *stuck*—

"You better come inside and have some oatmeal," Miss

Marple said. Her twinkling eyes were staring at me and Neely, and starting to look worried.

≈

Neely fainted at breakfast.

River was outside again, already finished eating his warm oatmeal with dried figs, cinnamon, cream, and butter. Finch and Canto hadn't come downstairs yet, and we had the place to ourselves. I told Neely what had happened the night before, with Canto, and River, and Brodie, and the Finnfolk boy.

He nodded, got up, and fainted.

I was down on the rug beside him, faster than the space between heartbeats. But Neely just sat up again, shrugged it off, and laughed. *Laughed.*

"You have to stop," I whispered. "You have to turn it off. It's killing you, Neely. You'll let River suck you dry until you fall apart and crumble into the wind."

Neely had another bruise under his right eye.

He was covered in them now.

River had noticed. Of course he had. I saw him staring at his brother over breakfast, eyes red and narrowed, the cuts on his neck looking raw and sore. Afterward he put a hand on Neely's shoulder and whispered something in his ear, but Neely only shook his head in response.

I knew River wouldn't want his brother to keep suffering for his sake . . . but I didn't think he was all that eager to go mad again, either. River, more than anyone, knew how bad things could get if he got his glow back.

Neely shook his head, and winced. "I can't. Look at him. Just look at him."

River stood in a foot of fluffy snow on the sidewalk outside, framed by the hotel window and a shaft of bright yellow sun that seemed to be shining just for him. He looked lean and comfortable and like he owned the place. Behind him, Gold Hollow was still and quiet in the sun and the fresh, deep snow. The whole damn scene was picture perfect and ready for its close-up.

"If I stop, Vi, he'll go back to being the sea king."

"Maybe he won't."

"He will."

"Maybe . . . maybe his madness was only Brodie's spark. And maybe it's worn off now of its own accord."

Neely laughed his rumbling laugh, though his eyes didn't join in. "Do you honestly believe that?"

I shook my head. Slowly.

But a mad River was better than a dead Neely.

I helped Neely to his feet and he groaned when I touched his back.

"It's going to kill you, Neely," I said again, and my voice went high at the end.

Neely didn't answer. He just breathed in and out, his hand on his ribs.

And then he fainted again.

He fell to the floor and I half caught him but I couldn't wake him up this time. I screamed his name and Neely's spine straightened in my arms, like someone stretching after setting down a heavy load. I felt something leave him then, felt it snap through the air. I looked outside, onto the porch, and River jerked, jerked like he'd been tugging at the end of a leash and it had finally broken. I saw it clear as day through the window. He spilled his coffee on the snow, and all over Neely's extra pair of boots.

River's expression shifted, and his eyes lost their glint. His arms stretched wide, and his chin pointed up to the sky and he went straight and tall and sea king again. He turned, and wandered off into the snow.

I leaned over Neely, grabbed his rich-boy sweater in my fists, pressed my nose into his neck, and let my brain scream and scream.

≈≈≈

Finch and Canto helped me carry Neely upstairs. We tucked him into bed and I waited for his eyes to open, any second, *come on, Neely,* but nothing. He was cold. Pale. Gray. Just like Finch after River drowned him and dumped him on the sand.

Canto kneeled by the bed and called out Neely's name and then patted his hand and her eyes were wet, and I guess mine were too. She looked at me, her red eyes meeting my red eyes. "Where is he?" she asked. "Where is River?"

I didn't answer.

"Where is he?" Canto asked again. "Violet, you need to find him. We'll stay here. Go."

I looked at Finch and his eyes were worried and serious and he nodded at me too. "Hurry, Violet."

I released my grip on Neely's sweater, one hand at a time. I slid off the bed and got to my feet.

"Don't let him die, Finch."

"I won't," Finch said, and meant it.

≈≈≈

I found River in the meadow.

He was stretched out on his back in the fluffy snow behind the old cars. A rusted yellow, a rusted black, and a rusted red, lined up before him like a congregation.

His sweater was on the ground beside him, a black lump in the white. And before he even said anything, I knew. It had started again. Already.

"Violet. There you are." River put his naked arms behind his beautiful head, and smiled up at me. And it wasn't the crooked smile. It was the mad, lost smile.

I was pretty familiar with both by now.

"You're lying half naked in snow. Aren't you cold, River? Don't you even feel it?"

"This is snow?" River lifted his head and looked around him. "I thought it was sand."

Another snowflake hit my cheek with a cold, wet plop. And then another.

I picked up River's sweater, brushed it off, reached down again, and held out my hand. River grabbed it, and I pulled him to his feet.

"Girl."

I turned. Wild Ann Boe stepped out from behind the old red car, her old green coat swinging against her calves. "You need to be careful, *girl*."

I didn't even answer her. I was watching the way River had perked up when she called out to me. Jaw clenched tight, posture erect and kingly. He stared down at Wild Ann over his nose and pointed his glow at her. I could feel it, feel a shift in the air between the two of them.

Her eyes started blinking, blinking fast.

I stepped between River and Boe, as if that would do any good.

But I guess it did because Wild Ann's gray eyes stopped blinking. Widened. She turned them right on me, and they opened up deep, like she was welcoming me to step inside.

"The Devil is holding your hand, *girl,*" she said. "Did you know?"

I froze.

A dark cloud passed overhead.

The sun was gone. It was dusky dark and suddenly the snow was pouring down.

I stood frozen, numb, my feet in the snow.

A raven cawed from somewhere far away, somewhere in the trees at the edge of town.

My wrists started throbbing.

You stop fearing the Devil when you're holding his hand.

Freddie had said that once.

And now here was this Colorado mountain woman standing in front of me, telling me that the Devil's hand was all up in mine.

Wild Ann turned to River, looked up at him, and seemed to forget all about me. Her eyes went blank. Dead. Her thin lips closed. River started humming and she joined him, humming in harmony, as if they were singing a duet, her high, him low. Humming, humming, humming out the nonsense sea sounds . . . the sound of *waves hitting skin, and the tide going in, and fish tails slapping and forest boys flapping . . .*

I let go of River's hand.

Wild Ann's eyes darted right to mine again, dead, dead,

dead. She stopped humming. "*Girl.* Did you know the Devil was following you? Did you know?"

And then she went back to humming with River.

And I just stood there, letting them.

≈

I saw the bookmobile first. Parked outside the Hollow Miner Hotel, bright red sides covered in mud and slush, the words THE ECHO LIBRARY BOOKMOBILE painted big and black and barely visible through puffs of snow.

And then I was running. Luke. Me. Bear hug.

I saw Sunshine while I was hugging my brother and smiled at her over his shoulder and she smiled right back.

"We barely made it, Vi," she said, slow and lazy like it was a fine summer's day out and not a storm roaring and picking up steam. Her blue scarf whipped in the wind. "I hope you appreciate it. Luke had to come. Made me steal the library's bookmobile. My parents are going to murder me—" Sunshine flinched, and put a hand to her head. "They're going to be really pissed off. So I hope it was worth it."

I let Luke go and squinted at him through the falling snow. God, it was good to see my twin brother again. It really was. "How did you know to come here?"

"After we left Riddle, we went home and checked on Jack and then talked to Sunshine's dad, who confirmed where you went based on the message you left. We barely made it before the storm. The roads were hell. Thank god Sunshine can drive like a guy."

"But what about the barn boy? It was Brodie, wasn't it?" I had to half shout against the roaring wind—it screamed in my ear and tore at my hair and clothes like some lusty drunk in a Robert Louis Stevenson alley.

"We got there too late. The barn boy was already gone. And the two girls who reported the story are missing. We thought he came here. Have you found him? Have you heard anything?"

River came up behind me and Luke's eyes shifted toward him.

I shook my head. "He's not here. It was just an old woman, spreading rumors."

Luke swore. He threw a few effs at the stormy sky, and then sunk down to sit on the snowy steps of the hotel. Sunshine went to his side and sat down next to him and put her head on his shoulder.

"It doesn't matter," I said. "It really doesn't matter. I'm just glad you're here. I was worried about you. Both of you."

"Ditto," Luke called out against the wind, meeting my eyes and giving me one of his rare genuine smiles. "I see you found River," he added, his eyes back on William

Redding III, on his long, uncut hair, snowflakes swirling around him and falling on his shoulders.

"Sort of," I said.

And then River started singing again, mouth open, head back . . . but his voice was drowned out by the storm.

≈≈≈

The blizzard raged outside.

Neely's fever raged inside.

I brought Luke and Sunshine and River upstairs, to Neely. River saw his brother stretched out on the bed, still as midnight. He kept humming, but he reached for my hand, his fingers closing around mine, still so damn familiar and comforting, despite *The Devil is holding your hand, girl,* despite everything.

Canto's eyes softened as she watched us standing there, our hands wrapped up together.

Neely slept on and Luke drew me into the hallway and made me tell him everything—Carollie, sea king, Neely, everything. And afterward he hugged me tight.

We spent the rest of the day inside, taking turns watching over Neely. His breathing was ragged and too quiet and his face was sunken and pale, and I felt broken, crushed, in my heart, in my soul, everywhere, damn it, damn it all.

The storm made twilight come early.

Miss Marple sent three shots of brandy up to Neely—

we told her he had the flu. Though she probably figured out that something more was going on.

The storm beat against the windowpanes and made them twitch and shake. The wind howled down the chimney.

"Violet," River said to me as I began to climb the stairs back to Neely's room, to relieve Finch and Canto from his side so they could eat supper.

I turned around.

And that was all it took. He didn't even need to touch me this time. He'd gotten past all that. Way past. Now he could do it just by saying my name.

My eyes closed. I heard River's heartbeat, each soft thrust of his pulse. I felt the rocking of the waves, rocking my body to and fro, to and fro. I heard *selkies slipping out of their skins, slick, squishy grins, discarded flippers, zip, zipping zippers, sea breaming, ships screaming, sleep, sleeping in the deep, deeping . . .*

I forced my eyes open. Slapped my hand down hard on the banister and squeezed.

Dizzy. Sick. Seasick.

This had been happening off and on since the cars and Wild Ann Boe. Supper was already a blur—the memory hazy around the edges, like it had been smeared with oil.

The feeling, the sea king feeling, the singing-in-the-sea feeling, was . . .

Everywhere.

In my head and in my heart and under my skin and in my bones.

River didn't want to be the sea king anymore. I know he didn't. Yet . . .

Neely woke up, sometime near midnight. He opened his eyes and I was the first to know since I was lying on the bed curled next to him.

"I'm okay, Vi," he said, just like that.

And I guess I should have gotten up and danced and sang for joy. But I didn't. I didn't move. I didn't say a word. Some deep part of me thought I was holding him together somehow, my arms around his chest and my cheek nestled into the hollow of his throat, and if I let go he would break into a million snowflake-sized pieces and float away on the winter storm.

"Violet," he whispered. His breath hit the back of my neck and my spine glowed, all the way down.

"Violet," he whispered again.

And he kept on whispering, secret, whispery things that made my damn heart swell, on and on until I thought it would burst right through my chest, cracking ribs on its way out . . .

And then.

"But none of that matters, Vi," he said. He kissed my

closed eyelids. "You need to be with River. He's too strong and he used too much glow and I can't control him anymore. But you . . . you cut through his glow-crazy and he tries to be better, for your sake." Neely shuddered, quick, quiet. "Go back to him. He needs you more than me."

And I thought my heart would shrivel up at this, go hard and tight and mean like a street-starved dog.

But it didn't.

It just kept . . . glowing.

I left Neely and went down the hall and climbed into bed with River.

River mumbled beside me, and he reeked of sea and salt again.

Freddie, what's going to happen to us? Neely and River and fevers and sea kings and drowned Roman Finnfolk and mountains and storms and my heart aches aches aches and where the hell is Brodie and . . .

And I guess that's when it occurred to me. The thought that scared the bejesus out of me, scared me out of my gosh darn Freddiedamned mind.

What if . . .

What if the entire time we'd been hunting down Brodie . . .

He'd been hunting down us?

CHAPTER 21

April

The first time.

In the wine cellar of Will's Manhattan townhouse.

My parents were both zozzled by six on rye whiskey and sweet vermouth. My mother tried to hoist me onto her friend's son between cocktails, a boy named Lucas White. He was heir to a shipping fortune and everything she wanted me to have.

I wore my jade necklace and my blue eyes and a white summer dress—one of three my mother had brought home from Paris that spring.

The Buccaneers. That's what people called

the Reddings. Will's parents were notorious in New York City for spiffy parties and bottomless cocktails and affairs and scandals and hushed-up bastard babies and dabblings in the occult. But I thought they were glamorous and mysterious and everything I wanted to be.

The Reddings and the Glenships and my parents, Klaus and Sadie Van Homan, moved in the same richie New York circles. We'd all grown up together, all us children, all stayed up too late at parties because our parents were too drunk to call the car around to take us home. We'd all tried Scottish whiskey and bathtub gin before we stopped believing in Santa Claus. All been sent off to boarding schools before we knew how to spell our last names.

Will had just been another boy, another son of my parents' friends. He pulled my hair, dared me to throw my shoes off the roof of our building, taught me to smoke, showed me how to mix a mean mint julep.

But suddenly he was fifteen. And I was fifteen. And everything had changed.

Mrs. Redding turned out the lights because it was time to contact the spirits and the women screamed with delight and the men hummed with drink and what was to come and Will found my hand in the dark and pulled me downstairs.

The party went on screaming above, louder now that the lights were out, and their footsteps tapped out a rhythm on the ceiling overhead. The wine cellar had a trick wooden panel to keep out the nosy cops. We climbed through it and it snapped shut behind us. It was big and dark and smelled of wood and grapes and cool basement air.

Will opened a bottle of gin. He drank, and then I drank, and at first I thought the burn was coming from the liquor sizzling its way down my throat, and maybe it was, but then Will's lips were on mine and everything was burning, burning . . .

I thought the burning was love and I thought back then that love trumped all.

And afterward, as we lay on the floor, naked and scared and stunned, Will took my hand and said, "What did we just do?"

And then he grabbed me and held me. My cheek touched his hair and his nose touched my milky green necklace, the one he would later take from me, and keep with him always, because it reminded him of this night.

After a while, a long while, we got dressed. But we still didn't go upstairs.

I sat there, worrying a bit about bastard babies, until Will took my hand again. I felt his heat shoot through me, into me, same as the gin that had burned down my throat.

"I want to do something for you, Freddie. Something only I can do. If . . . if you could see anything, anything in the world right now, what would it be?"

"Anthony," I said, not missing a beat.

Anthony used to sing me silly songs and swing me above his head and buy me little presents and tell me stories until I went to sleep. I loved him as much as any sister loved a brother. And he died like an animal, down in the mud and blood, in France.

Anthony.

Anthony.

In front of me. In his army uniform. One moment it was Will and then it was Anthony, smiling, his lips looking like he'd just said my name. I stood up. I cried out. I opened my arms to him . . .

He melted away. Dissolved into the bottles of wine. Like he'd never been. There was just Will. Only Will.

"I made that happen," Will said, kind of grand and proud. "I can make things happen. It started a few weeks ago, and I thought I was going out of mind, but now . . ."

I screamed.

And screamed.

My screams joined the screams of the women upstairs. No one heard me, except Will. I threw my arm back and brought it forward and hit Will across the face as hard as I'd ever hit anything in my life.

And then, after his nose finally stopped bleeding, after his shirt was covered in soft, wet red, I took him in my arms.

I told him everything was going to be all right.

I told him I loved him.

I told him to never, ever, ever do that thing again, the thing that he had done with Anthony. He promised he wouldn't. He promised me with his whole heart.

≈

The wind screeched through the window and I jerked out of sleep.

Raw and naked and not a stitch.

Both of us.

What had almost happened before, after the bully last summer, and again in the Lillian shack . . .

The water sliding between us, over us, under us, pushing us together, Violet White and the Sea King, like in the story, except there was no story, not yet, no story of shacks and sailors and shanties and shipwrecks and ravens and wrists and seaweed and sand . . .

It had almost happened again.

River was tucked into my side and he was smiling in his sleep and he had no idea what he was doing or what was going on.

And it was as I lay there, still as death, skin to skin with a mad Redding boy . . . that I put two and two together. That I connected the dots.

"You need to be careful, girl."

It was the scar. That was the first thing. I'd seen it when he was sleeping in front of the fire after being in the sea. A scar on the left side of his chest, right over his heart. I'd thought it was a shadow until I'd run my finger over it. He'd opened his eyes, and something . . . flickered . . . inside them, and inside me. But then a moment later I'd forgotten all about it. Almost like I was meant to.

"The Devil is holding your hand, girl."

The second thing.

In the hallway, after I'd crawled out of Neely's arms and was on my way to River's . . . someone called out my name. I turned to find him standing outside his door, shivering in a fresh flurry of snow that blew in from a crack underneath one of the Hollow Miner's windows.

"Neely woke up," I said.

Finch nodded, and smiled.

And then the smile disappeared.

"So you're going back to River."

"Neely asked me to," I said. "River needs me more."

He held my gaze, and then nodded. Slowly. "Forget about River, and forget about Neely. What do you want, Vi? Who is it that *you* need?"

I walked down the hall, right up to him. I put my hand on his heart, felt the pulse underneath. "You are so good. How did you get to be so good? My grandmother Freddie used to say that everyone has a little evil in them. But not you. Why is that?"

He took my hand, and his eyes were clear and bright and true. "Being good is as easy as being bad. You just have to put your mind to it."

And I laughed, a small, soft laugh, and had warm feelings about him . . .

Though something had seemed wrong, even at the time. Something I couldn't put my finger on.

The third thing.

Freddie's diary. Will becoming Freddie's dead brother and then becoming Will again. And River, turning into my mother in the guesthouse kitchen . . .

Pay attention, Vi. Don't sink back into it, don't let it in . . .

I turned over, shifting slowly so I didn't disturb River. I sat up, and pressed my toes into the cold, cold floor.

"Edith, you have the Devil sleeping in your hotel. Did you know?"

The storm beat against the windows and whined to be let in.

"Vi, where are you going?" River whispered.

"Nowhere," I lied. "I'm just going to get a shot of cognac from the bar. I'll be right back."

"Violet?"

"Yeah?" I looked at him over my shoulder.

"I love you." River looked at me. Straight at me. Sane as sunshine. "I love you. I love you as *certain obscure things are to be loved, in secret, between the shadow and the soul.*"

"That's one of my favorite poems," I said.

And then I dressed, left the room, and walked down the hall.

"Neely." He sighed in his sleep, and didn't move. I shook his shoulder, pressing my fingers into his soft, bare skin. How I hated to do it. He needed the sleep, damn it.

Shut up, Violet. You don't have a choice.

I shook him again. I felt the ridge of his scar under my fingertips. "Neely, wake up. It's important."

"What is it, Vi?" Neely yawned, and gave me a sleepy smile. "Did you hear the wolves howling again?" He reached out and pulled me down to the bed, sleepy, sleepy.

I cuddled up into his arms and thought about just staying there and not saying anything about anything. Ever.

"I need you," I whispered, a few minutes later.

There was a long pause. And then Neely sighed. "Is this about River?"

I shook my head. I put my hand to his face, my fingers on his new bruise. "Can you get dressed?"

Neely knew something was wrong. He'd woken up all the way now and the sleepy look was replaced with worry and strain. But he didn't ask any questions. He just slipped on his clothes and followed me down the hall.

We listened at the door.

Silence. No talking, no sheets rustling.

I didn't knock.

I turned the knob. Quiet, so quiet. Quiet as Poe and *The Tell-Tale Heart* and the *very, very slowly, so that I might not disturb the old man's sleep*.

I pushed open the door. Stepped one foot in, then another. I saw curly black hair lying next to red. Quiet, quiet, quiet, I walked over to them. Neely followed.

Eyes closed. Breathing soft. It was now or never. I pointed at the red hair, turned to Neely, and nodded.

He looked at me, uncomprehending. But he nodded back. He inhaled twice, short and quick. His eyes half closed in a wince and I felt the air sizzle around me.

I looked down. Down to Finch, sprawled on the bed, his arms around Canto.

At first I thought it was a trick of the eerie blue blizzard light outside, streetlamps reflecting off the snow.

Finch started to . . . shimmer. And then grow blurry. And then shimmer again.

I blinked. Rubbed my eyes.

Finch had . . . *stretched.*

He was a foot taller, toes sticking out of the blankets and touching the bed frame.

And his body was no longer Gene Kelly strong. It was skinny. Skin and bones skinny. Ichabod Crane and Uriah Heap skinny.

The red hair, though. That stayed exactly the same.

I pressed my fist to my mouth but I didn't scream. Neely put his arms around my waist and pulled me back into the corner of the room, into the shadows. "This whole time, *this whole damn time,*" I whispered, over and over. But it hadn't caught up to me yet, was still lying in wait, gathering its strength . . .

I saw Brodie's eyelids flutter. And then close again.

Finch was Brodie.

Had always been Brodie.

I felt sick, shivering, mucky, sweaty, sick. There was a roaring in my ears like I was underwater, drinking in the sea, like Roman, like Canto, like Finch—

Neely started to shake. His whole body, shaking like leaves on trees. And I thought maybe he was crying at first, but no, it was just the shaking. "He's my half brother. He tried to kill you. I should have known," he whispered. "He could have killed us at any time, could have killed you, could have killed River—"

I tried to picture myself holding one of the knives, the one I'd grabbed from the picnic basket before waking up Neely, tried to picture myself sticking it in, through skin, through muscle, between bone, ignoring the screams, and the flailing, and the blood, pushing back the fear, I had to hit his heart this time, I had to get it all the way in . . .

I couldn't do it.

I didn't have to stand over him, didn't have to see the red hair, to know.

I couldn't kill Brodie.

Because he wasn't just Brodie. He was Finch now too.

Remember. *Remember Sunshine and the bat and the blood on Jack's back and your gushing wrists and your lips on his . . .*

I slid out of Neely's arms.

I would do it.

I would.

Freddie, I'm going to do it.

I can't stop, I can't think, I can't let the fear fill me up, I can't let the doubt in, Neely is staring at me, he's still shaking, don't think about Neely, Vi, just go, go, go, red hair, don't look, don't look at Brodie's face, what if he looks like Finch, don't look, Vi, see his wrist? Look at his wrist, keep looking at it, slide the knife across, just slide it across, do it . . .

Now—

I did it. The knife slipped over his skin, like it was dancing, a thin red line . . .

. . . and then Brodie's eyes were open and he was screaming and Canto's eyes were open and she was screaming and everything was blur and chaos and Neely was there and I dropped the knife and scuttled backward, Neely beside me, our backs against the wall, like an execution, and Canto was sitting up and staring at Brodie and still screaming and then Brodie was staring at his wrist as the blood came and my only thought was, *What have I done? What the hell have I done?*

"You cut him." Neely's eyes weren't looking at me, only looking at Brodie, just Brodie. "Why didn't you ask me first? Damn it, Vi. *Why didn't you ask me first?*"

"Well, that's the million-dollar question, isn't it, brother." Brodie held his bleeding wrist in his left hand and then he was right there in front of me, naked from the waist up, River-style, and it made him seem even younger, somehow. The pajama bottoms hung limp on his skin and bones, and he was tall and lank and red hair, just like before, just like last summer . . . but he didn't have the cowboy hat and his drawl had faded and I didn't know what to think or who he was or what to believe.

"Hello there, Violet White. Long time no see. For you that is, not for me. I've been seeing you every day for a week." Brodie grabbed a thin white T-shirt from a drawer, wrapped it around his wrist, gritted his teeth, and pulled it tight with his left hand.

The boy who left me to die was standing in front of me. A boy who slit wrists and drove girls to suicide and turned my friends into rats and set people on fire and . . .

. . . and sacrificed himself to the sea in place of a girl he hardly knew.

Maybe Brodie would kill me now. Maybe he would kill me and make it stick.

"Which is the real one, Vi?" Neely whispered. "Which is the real one?"

And I didn't answer because I didn't know. I wanted to slap Brodie across the face, smash, palm to cheek, over and over, until he changed back into the forest boy, poof—

Canto was out of the bed now and watching Brodie, eyes vast, staring and staring and staring and looking more and more broken every damn second that passed.

I heard a new sound. A new scream. Not my own and not Canto's.

Sunshine.

She and Luke. Standing in the corridor. How long had they been there? They'd taken a room across the hall from Finch's. *They heard everything, everything since Brodie woke up howling after I slashed his damn skinny wrist.* Sunshine threw up on the floor in front of her. I saw it. I smelled it. And she was cradling her head and Luke was holding her in his arms and saying my name, over and over . . .

"So you figured it out." Brodie smiled at me.

And his smile was cocky and leering on the surface . . . but underneath it was calm and quiet.

How could it be both?

"Took you long enough, Vi. The scar . . . I couldn't quite

get rid of that, even with the spark. You cut me deep, you did, last summer. But hey, I cut you too, so I called it even. But here you are, at it again."

Brodie put his slashed arm in the air, and I could see red spots on the white shirt, the wound bleeding through. He began to spin around, but there were no boots this time, only his bare heels, and his heart didn't seem to be in it, and it wasn't remotely the same.

He stopped spinning. He came over to me. His left hand went to my chin, his fingertips touched my neck.

Neely's fists twitched. I saw them from the corner of my eyes. If he hit Brodie . . . *Don't hit Brodie, Neely* . . .

"You see, Violet, I'd about had all the fun I was going to have in Inn's End, and I was getting bored, when I came upon this boy in the woods. He had red hair just like me, so of course I was interested. I spied on him for a few days. Realized he was all alone, and that he spent a lot of time talking to the ghost of his dead grandmother. I learned plenty."

Brodie dropped my chin and winked at me in a pleasant, amiable way. "Finch wasn't afraid of my flock of ravens like the rest of the town. They wouldn't attack him for some reason, spark or no. And I have to say, it pissed me off. So finally I just strolled right up to him in the woods, and smashed a rock into his left temple. Down he went. Then I reached inside his head with my spark and . . . *squeezed.*" Brodie brought his hands up in front of my face, fists clenched. "I didn't know if it would work, but it did. I squeezed all his wits right out, squeezed them out until he was as slack-faced and stupefied and senseless as a whore on gin."

Brodie paused, as if taking time to enjoy the memory.

I felt Neely's fingers grab mine.

Luke held Sunshine in the hallway; she was white and limp and just . . . gone. Brodie glanced at them, and nodded, just to show he didn't care.

"So there I was," he continued, his eyes lighting up, right up, "laughing and whooping and kicking Finch's body in and just, you know, reveling in my success, when I heard those damn Inn's End–ers approaching. Quick as a cheater's wink, I sparked myself up to look like Finch. I ran back to his cabin and hunkered down nearby and let them catch me. After all, I figured I could always undo it later, and I wanted to see what would happen anyway. See if they would turn on their own."

Brodie laughed. And it was fast and mad but also sane and soft and *how could it be both at the same time?*

"And then by God I catch sight of you and Neely in the crowd at the church. It couldn't have worked out better if I'd wished for it. All along I'd planned to head back to

Citizen Kane after Inn's End, planned to spark myself up to look like Luke or Jack and see what happened. Granted, I probably couldn't have kept it up for as long—this shape shifting works better the more I look like the person I'm shifting to. Still, that would have been a fun few days, no doubt." He paused. Smiled. "Then I find out you two are heading to Carollie, and, you know, perfect. I'd just come from there. I drowned some hotshot local boy and then I sparked up River and drowned him too. I left the hotshot dead but I brought River back. I knew the two of us Reddings would work together someday. It was fate."

Brodie drowned River.

River died like Finch, and came back . . .

The blood from Brodie's wrist had soaked through the shirt and was dripping on the floor now, little plops, every so often, but enough, enough.

I'd hurt him more than he was letting on.

Please let that be true . . .

No, no, I don't want that to be true at all . . .

"You didn't seem to like my mad cowboy all that much, Vi." Brodie walked across the room and leaned against the door frame, five feet from Luke and Sunshine. He stretched, and looked even taller. "None of you did. So I thought I'd try something different. I aim to please."

"But you let yourself get drowned," Canto whispered,

and she shook her head, shook it again and again, her black curls swishing across her shoulders. "You let River *drown* you."

"I'm a Redding. Nothing can stop me. Not one damn thing." Brodie paused, and his green eyes . . . flickered. "Besides, I'd already been drowned once. River drowned me before I left Carollie and went to Inn's End. I let him. His glow was different after the big blue sucked out his life and I wanted to see if death would change my spark too. And it did."

Brodie shimmered . . . shifted . . .

And he was Finch again, just for a second, *one, two, three.* Gone.

"You know," he said, his voice sounding like Finch's, though the mouth it came out of was Brodie's, "I always wondered what it would be like to be part of the Citizen Kane group after watching you all last summer with your bonfires and your espresso . . . I've had the time of my life these last few days. Better than sparking people. Better than burning people up. Better than standing in the forest on a clear autumn night with the moon in the sky and the wolves at my feet and the smell of wood smoke in my hair . . .

"But I guess the joke's on me." Brodie held up his dripping wrist. He stared at it for a second, and kept on talking.

"I took on that kid's looks and his personality came too. Didn't know that would happen. My spark changed when I was down in the deep, when the sea held my life in its palm. Which came first: the spark or the Brodie? I'm not scared, I'm a fucking Redding, except my spark, that might scare me, sometimes it scares me. My ma said I was born with a Great Rage inside me, but Finch made that disappear . . . I always thought skinny is as skinny does, but sometimes, sometimes I forget I'm not Finch. Here Canto is the new Sophie, and River is as mad as a damn hatter and four times as interesting as he ever was, and I have all my options in front of me, everything I ever wanted . . . and yet all I want to do is just . . . keep on being . . . Finch . . ."

There were red drops all over the floor and Brodie dropped his arm, *thud,* like it was made of lead, and his breaths were odd, uneven, weak.

"And then Neely starts getting his bruises," he added, his voice sounding less and less Brodie and more and more Finch, quiet, serene. "Got himself his own spark. That was a surprise. I figured I'd have to change my plans now, now that . . . but I couldn't seem to stop being Finch, I . . ." He looked at Canto.

"Did you kill the real Finch?" Canto asked, and her words were shaking but her body wasn't, not anymore.

"Did you kill him all the way, like you killed Roman?"

Brodie was wheezing now. He still leaned against the door frame, but it wasn't a cocky, bored lean. It was like he couldn't stand up on his own. "What do you think, kids? I let Finch take over for too long. It's time for some real fun. Any requests? I was thinking of setting Echo against Jack and Sunshine, for starters, the whole town, make people think they're *infected,* something grotesque and whimsical, you know, something that would end in panic, and blood . . ."

Brodie kept talking, even as his face went whiter, even as his hands began to shake, dangling at the ends of his skinny arms like dead leaves on dying branches . . .

"Or I could turn myself into Freddie and start haunting you, Violet. I can just imagine your face, waking up to find Freddie in your room, telling you to do evil things to the people you love. I have so many ideas. I want River to kill Luke in a duel. I want Canto to murder a child in cold blood. I want . . ."

Brodie coughed, and dropped to his knees.

And then River was in the hallway behind him, pushing Luke and Sunshine out of the way, and he was reaching down, putting his hands on Brodie's head, one on each side, and River screamed, *Do it now, Neely,* and Sunshine screamed, *Squeeze, River, squeeze his wits out, end it . . .*

. . . and Brodie burst out of River's grip and was on his feet and a blur of red hair and a skinny body flying by and then he was out the window and into the snowstorm and jumping down from the roof and landing in the soft white and back up again and running, running, running, down through the hotel, all of us, out the door, following the footprints, ten long, skinny toes, drops of blood on the snow, like back in Inn's End, back in Pine's cemetery, right through the tall pines, right to the edge of an alpine lake, thin ice, newly frozen.

We lined the edge, panting, shivering, bare feet.

We watched the flash of red, moving, already halfway across the lake.

The moon came out and the wind died down, whoosh, all at once, hush, hush.

The first crack was thin, weak. A pop, a squeeze.

The second crack was low. Deep.

And the red grew smaller, smaller, smaller by the second . . .

I put my right foot on the ice, flinched at the cold, brought my left foot forward . . .

. . . Luke and Neely, hands on my arms, yanking me back . . .

"Let me go." I shivered and shaked and strained. *"If he gets away, we'll never be able to see anyone, anyone at all, without thinking it's Brodie, sparked up, lying, spying, in the*

shadows, everywhere, he'll come to Citizen Kane and pretend to be us, torture us, and it'll just go on and on—"

The ice groaned again, snarled, popped, rang out into the night—

A streak of brown hair.

River.

He was flying, feet barely touching the ice, chest out, heart first, closer, closer, gaining, gaining, he reached out, almost, almost—

He's going to do it, he's going to save us, I know he is, Freddie, see, it's different, it's not like you and Will, River is—

The ice creaked again.

River was there, running, reaching, right arm stretched, grabbing Brodie's hair in his fist—

And then . . . gone.

Snap, blink, gone.

But the red kept running.

Neely howled.

I screamed.

Neely and me, bare feet hitting the ice with a sting, but he was too far, we'd never make it, he was too far away, he'd freeze to death, drown, icy chunks filling up his lungs—

The red turned. I saw it through the blur of dark forest and night sky and snow. It turned around, and came back.

And by the time Neely and me reached the hole, the

black hole that had swallowed River up, Brodie had him out again, dripping body spread wide across the ice. He breathed and pumped and breathed and pumped and moved right aside so Neely could take over and then Brodie's arms were around me and they felt thick and strong and I clung to him and he held me tight and the blood-soaked shirt around his wrist pressed into my neck and the red dripped down my chest and I didn't care, didn't care at all . . .

River coughed and sputtered and shook and opened his eyes . . .

And Neely was saying, *River, thank God, thank God* . . .

. . . and then River was on his feet. He pulled Brodie from my arms . . .

And he shoved him down to his knees, on the ice, crack, crack, and River put his wet, shivering hands in Brodie's red hair and I thought there might be strikes of lightning or bursts of flames or clouds of smoke but there was nothing, nothing . . .

Nothing until Brodie fell backward, all the way, onto the ice, red hair fanning out, quiet, not moving. Still.

CHAPTER 22

IT LOOKED SO beautiful. It looked so where-have-you-been-all-my-life.

It looked like home.

Citizen Kane.

We drove thirty hours straight, pulling over to the side of the road only once so Neely and Sunshine could sleep.

A blur. A blur of trees and snow.

We put Brodie in the back of the bookmobile. He still hadn't woken up, but we wanted to be sure. We wedged him in between the piles of books that had fallen to the floor in the cross-country trek.

I swept a lock of red hair off his forehead, and goose bumps broke out across my skin. And then I moved his arms so he would be more comfortable. They were long and bony and Brodie-skinny . . . but when they'd held me on the frozen lake they'd felt strong and forest-boy.

He'd come back.

He'd saved River.

Neely had stitched up his wrist, and it was clean and bandaged tight, and if Brodie never woke up that wouldn't be the reason why.

Did we even want Brodie to wake up?

Who knew.

The spark. The glow.

It made the whole damn world spin upside down and walk backward and nothing made much sense anymore.

Nothing except how much I already missed Finch.

It was three in the morning when we arrived in Echo. Neely parked the car in the exact same spot that River had on that day last summer, by the front steps. Sunshine parked the bookmobile right behind it. We stood there in front of my home, sleepy, dazed, stiff, the cold hitting us like a smack after the warmth from the car.

I contemplated kissing the snowy ground in front of the Citizen, I did. It was melodramatic, but I get that way when I'm tired.

Still, the smell of the sea. The sound of it in my ears.

We went inside and stood in the foyer and kind of swayed in that way you do when it's really late at night and you've been traveling in a car, drifting in and out of sleep.

Neely and Sunshine, who'd done all the driving, all of it, looked like hell. Neely was so tired he was leaning against the wall for support, his head rubbing against the sagging art deco wallpaper.

I never knew that the Citizen had its own smell. I guess you have to leave for a while to know that about your house. I breathed in and it was old books and Freddie's French perfume and coffee and pine trees and . . . vanilla, for some reason. It was the smell of me, and my life.

I thought we might wake someone up with all our sleepy bumbling and swaying, but no one came down to investigate, not even Jack, who was a light sleeper.

Luke and Neely and River carried Brodie upstairs and put him in one of the Citizen's guest rooms. His tall body stretched all the way from one end of the bed to the other. His face, in sleep, was peaceful. Quiet. Calm.

My parents' bedroom was empty.

I found Pine sleeping on the sofa in Jack's room.

So she'd come to Citizen Kane after all.

I kneeled down beside her. I touched her arm and her eyes flew open.

"*It's not Finch,*" she said. "They found the real Finch in the forest, in a deep sleep, it's not Finch who went with you, who you rescued, I came to warn you, I came all the way to warn you—"

"It's okay, it's okay," I whispered. "I know. We figured it out. It was . . . someone else, pretending to be Finch, but it's all right now. It's all going to be okay."

Jack yawned then and sat up and saw me and saw me next to Pine and saw Pine's look of relief.

"She hitchhiked all the way," he said, rubbing sleep from his eyes and flashing a proud smile. "She'd never left Inn's End or the forest before, but she came all the way here on her own to warn you. Isn't she something?"

≈

"I crushed him." River ran his hands through his hair. "I crushed him from the inside out, like he crushed Finch. I didn't even know I could do that."

It was a sunny winter's day, the sky looking all the more blue for the white snow beneath it, my house looking all the more beautiful for how long I'd been away.

My parents were gone. They'd hopped a plane to Italy, according to Jack, off to hunt down their muse again. They didn't mention when they were coming back.

I was used to it.

Luke, River, Neely, and me stood in a half circle in the red guest room, yellow sun streaming in the three big fat windows with their view of the sea.

Sunshine said she wouldn't step foot inside the Citizen until Brodie was gone. She went home the night before and hadn't come back, not even to get the bookmobile.

"She'll change her mind," Luke said.

But I wasn't so sure.

Brodie had lost a lot of blood, but that wasn't the reason he was so pale and still and empty, with his eyes open and blinking but nothing in them, just like Gianni and Sunshine's parents and the islanders on Carollie and all the glowed up, sparked up people I'd seen since River first came to my damn town.

Yes, Brodie had opened his eyes, sometime in the night. But there was nothing in them. No spark of intelligence. They were blank as the sky on a hot summer day.

"He was already weak from Vi slashing his wrist," River added. He took his hands out of his hair and started tapping his fingers on one of the bedposts. "And then I went in with my glow and I squeezed . . . it felt like squishing a rotten apple in my fist." River paused. "But it also felt like stomping on a bright red butterfly . . ."

"You saved the damn day, River," Luke said, eyes half full of worship again, like they had been on the first day he met River, last summer, in the guesthouse.

But River didn't look like he saved the damn day. He seemed . . . thoughtful. Thoughtful and unsure and a bit lost. No arrogance. No sly smile. No nothing of the old River at all.

I looked at Brodie, took in his green eyes and his red hair and the unnerving, lifeless, still, still, still.

"He saved you from drowning," I said to River, quiet. "He drowned you on Carollie and then brought you back and then you were drowning in Colorado and he saved you again."

River nodded. "I guess that was the lingering forest boy in him."

"Finch is still in there somewhere," I whispered. "He is. I can feel it. Feel him."

"Brodie will need to be looked after," River said. "We can't just leave him like this."

"I'll take care of him." Pine stepped into our little half circle, her white-blond hair sweeping her shoulders, her thin arms straight at her sides. She had a scarf on, a silk scarf of a soft blue that she'd no doubt found in the attic. She looked half naive, and half sophisticated somehow. It suited her really well. "I took care of my father, after he got sick and lost his wits. I don't mind."

"Maybe you should," I said.

She looked at me, and shrugged her tight shrug. "It's got to be done and I know how to do it."

River crooked-smiled at her, and leaned his panther

hips against the dresser. "Where did this girl come from? She's like an angel sent from heaven, here to help us in our time of need." And then River waved his hand in the air, in a circle.

That gesture . . . it reminded me of someone.

Brodie.

It reminded me of Brodie.

What if . . . what if River had taken on a bit of Brodie when he glowed him into a vegetable, just as Brodie had taken on Finch when he put him in a coma and then sparked himself up as the forest boy . . .

If you think about that, Vi, you'll go mad. Just push that back and forget about it . . .

"I wish you'd killed him, sis. I do. " Luke put his arm around me and looked so worried it broke my damn heart a little bit. "What if he wakes up and nothing's changed and he's still the mad Brodie from last summer? What then?"

I met my brother's eyes. "If Brodie wakes up and he's still very much Brodie, with no trace of Finch at all, then . . . then we're no worse off than we were before we found him in Inn's End."

Luke paused. And then nodded. "I still wish you'd used your knife on Brodie's heart instead of his wrist. I wish you sliced it in two and stopped it dead. Even if he saved River.

Brodie tried to kill you. He almost did. I don't care if he's got a new spark or he's un-witted or lobotomized or half Finch. I don't like that he's here."

"You wouldn't say that, not if you knew." Neely was by the windows, the sunshine making his bruises sing, up and down his arms, over his neck, everywhere. "Not if you'd known Finch."

"How can a person be so good and bad at the same time?" I asked, out loud. "How is that possible?"

But no one answered me because no one knew.

≈≈≈

We went down to the kitchen for breakfast. All except River, who said he wanted to stay with Brodie for a while, and Canto, who was buried in some corner of Citizen Kane, mourning Finch, and Roman. Neely made coffee on the stove and suddenly looked tall and pink-cheeked and clear-eyed and a whole lot better despite the bruises. I nestled up next to him on the counter and let my arm brush his as I whisked Dutch pancake batter. Luke held the cast iron for me to pour it in while Pine and Jack took turns twisting oranges over the little glass squeezer.

The room smelled like joe and juice and melted butter and snow.

Every time Jack caught sight of me he grinned.

I'd missed him, that long week I was gone.

"Isn't she pretty," Jack whispered to me, standing on tiptoe so he could reach my ear. "Isn't Pine pretty?"

And she did look pretty. She was wearing some of my old clothes, which were Freddie's old clothes, plus the blue attic scarf. I watched her for a second, standing in the center of my yellow kitchen, her blond hair and her gray eyes and no one knowing much about her, not yet. It was so strange to see her in the Citizen's kitchen, this girl from the hidden, grim Inn's End. It was like seeing a figure from a nightmare, up and making breakfast in your kitchen the next morning.

"She said she's going to stay here, and go to school, and on weekends I'm going to teach her how to paint," Jack added.

"Good," I said. And meant it.

Luke put sliced bananas and maple syrup on the puffed-up pancake, and we ate standing at the table. The winter wind howled through the window cracks, but the kitchen was warm from the oven and all the people and it couldn't touch us.

River came down in the middle of our breakfast. I saw a flash of red behind him.

He told his half brother to sit down on the yellow kitchen sofa, and Brodie did it, just sat and stared. River went to the stove to pour himself a cup of coffee.

I watched River. We all did, out of the corners of our eyes. Him and Brodie. We waited for what would happen next, like a pot about to boil, or a bomb ticking down, or a record on the last song.

I remembered back to last summer, to that first day. River had made me eggs in a frame in this very kitchen . . . and then asked me to curl up next to him and take a nap on the yellow couch. I still didn't know if I'd done it because he'd used the glow on me, or if I'd done it just because he was River, a mysterious stranger who knew how to cook almost better than he knew how to lie.

Both maybe.

CHAPTER 23

Brodie wandered into my bedroom one night. I woke up and found him standing at the end of my bed, staring down at me, tall, gaunt, red hair glowing in the moonlight like it was lit from within.

But when I got up and took his arm he followed me back to the red guest room meek as a lamb.

Sometimes I thought I could feel evil coming off of him, invisible and subtle but potent all the same, like the scent of something rotting in the garbage, underneath all the pleasant kitchen smells. He slept when he was told to sleep, ate food when he was given it, seemed nothing but a biddable shadow.

And yet . . . I was worried. I was.

Pine was often at Brodie's side, when she wasn't in

school or with Jack. Walking around Citizen Kane meant finding Pine and Brodie in corners, white-blond and red, tall and tiny, neither talking.

Sometimes I thought about leading Brodie outside, across the road, to the cliffs, gentle, gentle, shove, shove, over he goes . . .

But then, in the right light, Brodie would . . . shimmer. Shimmer in a Finch way.

One day he was standing by the front door with Pine, limp and still as she dressed him for his daily walk outside. That's when I saw it. Brodie had a dimple. A dimple in his left cheek, a little dip that hadn't been there before.

I felt a little better. Maybe I shouldn't have, but I did.

Canto left.

"I'm going to find Finch," she said. "The real Finch. If he lives. If he isn't a vegetable, like Brodie. I'm going to find him."

I tried to warn her. Tried to get her to change her mind. Even Pine pulled her aside and told her that the last time she'd seen Finch he was in a sleep so deep no one could wake him. But Canto would do what Canto wanted to do. I packed her a picnic basket full of food and gave her maps and a pair of warm mittens and a bear hug.

"Neely can drive you," I said.

"No, I'd rather walk. Really. I'll take the train to that

university town in Virginia and hitch from there." Canto stood in the doorway with her curly black hair blowing in the winter wind and the ocean behind her like she was posing for a Leonardo.

Except I saw the fragile look in her eyes.

"There's a chance Finch will wake up and be himself again," I said. "There's always a chance."

But what I didn't say was, *If Finch can wake up, then Brodie can too.*

"If he's there I'll find him and bring him back to Captain Nemo and make him get better." She paused. "Roman's dead. But if I can still save Finch, then I have to try." Canto put her hand on her heart like she was pledging allegiance, or like she was keeping it from splitting in half. She gave me a fierce smile. "Be careful."

"I'm not scared of Brodie," I said, though I was.

"That's not who I meant." She stared at me for a second, a long second, and then turned and went down the steps.

I watched her walk off, all the way until the trees swallowed her up, just her and her suitcase on their way to the little Echo train station at the other end of town.

Neely was next. He found me in the kitchen, making espresso shortbread with Jack.

"I'm leaving," he said, and the second he said it I let my breath out. I hadn't realized I'd been holding it.

Neely and I had been walking circles around each other for days.

I knew he was going to leave. Somehow, I just knew.

"I'm heading off to find that barn boy and the two missing girls," Neely said. "I heard something on *Stranger Than Fiction* and I'm going to Canada. I think the barn boy could be another one of my half siblings. And if so, then I'm going to find him, and I'm going to help him. Before he turns into Brodie. Or River."

Jack looked up from stirring the batter, and his eyes were wide and very, very young. "Maybe those girls went with him because they wanted to. Maybe the barn boy is good. Maybe he's like you, Neely."

Neely just smiled, and it was a sad, un-Neely smile.

Neely was leaving.

I stared at the white flour that covered my blue cooking dress and then I closed my eyes and Neely put his arms around me and I let him. He whispered *I wish it had turned out differently* in my ear. And I felt the choking thing you feel, the one that comes even if you're not a crier.

Later that night, I went to him. I walked right past River's door and went to Neely's.

"I thought you'd never come," he said, and his long arms were around me, pulling me down to him, down onto the bed. His lips went to my neck and his hands to my waist.

Just for a few seconds, and then just a few more.

I thought of the horses.

On the beach, sand flying, reveling in each and every breath.

I reached up and wove my fingers into the roots of Neely's blond hair and gripped it tight and pulled his face down to mine and . . .

. . . and then I was on the beach, running like the horses, my heart screaming with the joy of it all, and I was alive, I was so damn alive, not afraid, not glowed up, not confused, just alive, alive, alive . . .

"What is it, Vi?" Neely asked, later, a lot later. After I'd stopped turning my head so he could reach another part of my neck, stopped gripping his naked lower back, stopped moving my hips with his.

"Neely, I need you to do something for me."

"Anything."

My insides sang out at the yearning I heard behind his voice. "Come back," I said. "Come back to Citizen Kane. No matter what."

"I will. I promise."

Neely kept his promises, unlike River. So I trusted him.

So I let him go.

≈

River.

I was going to stay by his side, damn it. Unlike Freddie, with Will. I wasn't going to be scared away. Wasn't going to turn my back on him.

Maybe River was the one I should push over the cliff.

Or drown in the sea.

Maybe it would help. Maybe one more time would do the trick.

I don't mean that, Freddie. Not really. . . .

River was sane again. Mostly. Maybe his madness finally wore off, like Neely always said it would. Or maybe the icy claws of the frozen lake cut it out of him. I don't know. He wasn't the sea king now, but he wasn't the sly, carefree River of last summer, either. He was distant with me, with everyone but Jack, and he drifted in and out of Citizen Kane, quiet, mysterious, always so damn mysterious, disappearing for a few days to who knew where and then strolling back again like it was nothing.

But River had been drowned and starved and sea king–ed and then almost drowned again and a person didn't recover from that overnight. I'd stay by William River Redding III. I would. Because Neely would want me to. And because I knew he would get better, if given enough time. I felt it in my bones.

Even if River still walked around without a shirt on.

Even if he refused to wear shoes half the time . . .

Even if I caught him staring at the sea in the sea king way, three times a day.

Even if I found him singing sea songs in some dusty corner of the library, or on some dusty sofa in the attic, when he didn't think anyone could hear him.

Even if he spent his days reading or painting with Jack or cooking instead of attending school or going home and dealing with his father.

Even if he mostly slept in the guesthouse but still crawled into my bed every so often, and I let him, let him put his arms around me and bury his face in my hair and sleep like that until dawn, never anything more now, just sleeping.

Even if I stumbled upon River standing still under a blue sky and humming the sea sounds with Jack, more than once.

Even if I opened the door to Brodie's room and found River leaning over the bed, and he'd shut his mouth, quick, as if he and Brodie had been in the middle of a conversation that he didn't want me to hear.

≈≈≈

We were drinking hot caramel milk from a thermos in the Echo cemetery, in front of the Glenship mausoleum.

Right near the spot where Jack had watched for the Devil, right near the spot where River had glowed a bully into his own train-smashed death in a ditch.

Luke, Pine, Jack, Sunshine, and I had come to pour blood on the mausoleums.

I took the second stainless-steel thermos from Jack's hands, opened it, and looked inside.

The blood looked black in the dying light, but it still smelled red.

A breeze blew in from the ocean below. Suddenly everything smelled like the sea and the blood scent was gone. I breathed in deep and felt better.

"I had to pull a River to get it," Jack confessed. He shrugged his shoulders. They seemed stronger, broader, than before I'd left. He was getting older. "I had to promise the butcher I wasn't trying to fake my own death, like with Huck Finn. I guess butchers are onto this trick. I told him we were Scottish and we wanted to make blood sausage."

I winked at Jack, quick, sly, River-style. "Well, the butcher never would have believed the truth anyway."

I held out the thermos to Luke. "Do you want to go first?"

Luke smiled his old condescending smile. "No way, sister. I've come to watch, not participate. I want to see how far you'll take this crazy plan."

Pine frowned. She was wearing the scarf I'd given her in Inn's End, and she tucked her small, pointed chin into it, and looked at the ground.

Jack scowled. "It's not crazy, Luke. Pine told me she poured blood on the stones in Inn's End and prayed they would find Brodie. And they did. Even though he looked like Finch at the time, it was still Brodie, and they still found him."

"That doesn't make it any less barbaric. Or crazy." Luke looked at me. "If anyone catches us we'll never live it down. We'll be the crazy blood-wielding Whites forever."

"Shut up, Luke," I said. And held out the thermos.

"Yeah, shut up, Luke," Jack said.

Pine looked at Jack, and then my brother, and smiled. "Pour the damn blood, Luke."

"Fine." Luke grabbed the thermos from me. He looked at Sunshine. "I knew we should have just gone to your house instead."

But he filled up the thermos cap with blood, walked to the Glenship mausoleum, and threw it across the door. It splattered and dripped, red ribbons bleeding into the snow. Luke knocked the cup against the stone to get the last drops, and then handed the thermos back to me. "Now what?"

We went on down the line, each of us throwing the red red red at the wood and stone of the tomb, Jackson

Pollocking it with blood instead of paint. And then we went to the White mausoleum and did the same thing.

I splattered the last drops over the letters "Rose Redding," and then the whole damn thing from top to bottom was dripping red. I motioned for Pine to make her prayer.

"And thou shalt slay the swine, and thou shalt take his blood, and sprinkle it on the stones."

"Please keep away the spark," Pine added, a second later. "Please keep away the glow."

"Please keep away the burn," I added. "Please help Neely on his Redding brat hunt. Help him find the two missing girls. And then make him come back home, to Citizen Kane."

And after it was all done, and the top screwed back on the thermos, I told Pine and Jack and Luke and Sunshine about River, talking to Brodie.

"Do you think he can read Brodie's thoughts?" Jack asked. He sipped the burnt-sugar-tasting caramel milk and tried not to the let the worry show through his sweet, freckled face.

I grabbed a fistful of Freddie's skirt and squeezed it between my fingers. Something I used to do, last summer. Something I hadn't done in a while. "What if River couldn't bring himself to do it, not all the way? What if Brodie's mind is still alive and aware and raging somewhere inside, somewhere hidden? Somewhere that can't be found without a River-ish *X marks the spot* treasure map?"

The five of us leaned against the Glenship mausoleum, and a few quiet minutes ticked by . . . but then Jack made a joke about pirates and Pine laughed and Luke said there was a treasure map in the attic, inside one of the trunks shoved into the back corners . . . and then all of us went home to the Citizen, Sunshine too, and climbed to the top floor and dug around in the dust and clutter and creep until it got so late we ended up falling asleep in the middle of the floor on a pile of moth-bitten clothes that someone hadn't put away, probably me.

And the last thought I had before I drifted off, my cheek rubbing against an old velvet cloak, was that everything was going to be all right in the end. Luke was on his back, snoring to wake the dead, and Sunshine had her head in the crook of his arm, and Jack was curled up with Pine, and they were both using the same tall Marie Antoinette wig for a pillow, and maybe Finch would still be alive and maybe River was half sane again but still a little bit of a sea king and maybe Brodie wasn't entirely un-witted and maybe River was talking to him in secret . . .

But. But Neely was going to come back soon. He'd promised.

And meanwhile I was going to count my lucky stars and keep thinking of those wild horses.

Freddie used to say that life could be safe, or it could be interesting, but it couldn't be both. I was content with the path I'd taken, no matter what, hands down, no question. I really was.

I really, really was.

Acknowledgments

Jessica Garrison, for every damn thing ever.

Molly Sardella & Jessica Shoffel, Bri Lockhart, and everyone else at Penguin, with a special shout-out to Jill Bailey, Colleen Conway, Biff Donovan, and all the other kickass field sales reps. You are brilliant. All of you.

Joanna Volpe, for the frozen lake, for sneaking into the cemetery, for being the best damn agent a girl could ask for.

Everyone else at New Leaf Literary, especially Danielle and Kathleen.

Kendare Blake.

Melissa Marr.

Nova Ren Suma.

The library girl who asked me to sign an old copy of Byron.

Alison Cherry, for giving me a lock of her red, red hair.

James, Cindi, and Junior Warburton, for the Friday the thirteenth camping trip, complete with middle-of-the-night screaming.

H. P. Lovecraft.

Erin Bowman.

Megan Shepherd.

To my butler, Henry, for his years of service, and for providing the clue that solved the mystery.

To my Gravedigging Mentor. You always know just what to say. And where to dig.

Oscar & Finn.

Nate, for the bottle of poison.

April Genevieve Tucholke

is a full-time writer who digs coffee, redheaded heroes, attics, and discussing poison at the breakfast table. *Between the Devil and the Deep Blue Sea,* her widely praised debut novel, is the first book in this duet. She and her husband—a librarian, former rare-book dealer, and journalist—live in Oregon at the edge of the forest.

Visit April on
Twitter @NightOwlAuthor and at
AprilTucholke.com